I'm Emma:
I'm a Quint

STELLA PEVSNER

I'm Emma: I'm a Quint

Clarion Books
New York

Clarion Books
a Houghton Mifflin Company imprint
215 Park Avenue South, New York, NY 10003
Text copyright © 1993 by Stella Pevsner

Printed in the U.S.A.
Library of Congress Cataloging-in-Publication Data

Pevsner, Stella.
    I'm Emma: I'm a quint / by Stella Pevsner.
      p. cm.
    Sequel to: Sister of the quints.
    Summary: Thirteen-year-old Emma, one of a set of quintuplets,
struggles to maintain her individuality as she attends acting class,
prepares for her half-sister's wedding, and auditions for a movie.
    ISBN 0-395-64166-7
    [1. Quintuplets—Fiction.   2. Brothers and sisters—Fiction.
3. Individuality—Fiction.   4. Acting—Fiction.]   I. Title.
PZ7.P44815Iam   1993
[Fic]—dc20   92-36952
                                                     CIP
                                                     AC

VB   10   9   8   7   6   5   4   3   2   1

To Mary Applegate

CHAPTER 1

*A*s I walked down the hall I heard my sister Alice say, "I shouldn't even be talking to you."

She was on the telephone, hunched over a little, and so naturally I strained to hear more.

"Because our parents don't want us to," Alice said. She glanced up, saw me, and plopped her hand over the mouthpiece. "Go away," she whispered. She looked flustered.

"What's wrong?" I asked.

"Nothing." She hunched over the phone a little more. I went to the stairs, but hung over the banister to listen.

"I don't think it would do any good," Alice said. "They don't like publicity of any kind."

It was something about our being quints, then.

After a bit she said, "All right, I'll try. Listen, I've got to hang up now."

"What was that all about?" I asked the second she put down the phone.

"The usual," Alice said. She looked at herself in the

hall mirror and lifted her hair with her fingers. "I think I should go blonder. I'm beginning to fade."

"You know we're not supposed to talk to reporters."

"This wasn't a reporter."

"No? Then what?"

"Emma, you're a real drag sometimes."

That was an old Alice technique. I ignored it.

"Who, then? If it wasn't a reporter . . ."

Alice gave a huge sigh. "All right." She whirled toward the stairs, dodged around me, and raced upward. I stayed right behind her.

"A TV guy," she said. "He just wanted some shots for later on. When we graduate."

She had reached her room by now. She went in and slammed the door shut. I opened it and followed her in.

"Do join me," Alice said. "Come right on into my private room. Don't be shy."

It was Beth's room, too. Beth was just coming out of the bathroom, toweling her hair.

"I did it," she said.

"EEEEeee!" Alice squealed. "Let me see!"

"You can't tell when it's wet," Beth said. "I hope it's not noticeable. Dad will kill me."

"If you don't want it to be noticeable, why bother to bleach it?" I asked.

"It's not bleached, just color highlighted," Beth said. "And how did you know, anyway?"

"Oh, please." I flopped onto Alice's bed, grabbed her ancient teddy bear, and pulled out some fur. Since everyone had been doing this for years, Buffy was almost bald all over. "All you two have been talking about for months is becoming these hot blond babes."

Alice and Beth exchanged looks that said *Isn't it sad?* If they'd come right out and said *Emma's jealous because her hair is too dark and there's nothing she can do about it until she's really old and away from our parents*, I'd have told them I didn't want to be a blond bimbo. But since they hadn't actually said it, I switched back to the other subject.

"Alice has been talking to a TV guy," I told Beth, turning onto my stomach and using Buffy as a pillow.

"Yeah?" Beth stopped toweling her hair. "What did he want?"

"The usual. Story and pictures."

Beth's eyes widened. "You didn't . . ."

"Of course not." Alice leaned down and jerked Buffy out from under me. "You think I'm nuts?"

"You going to tell the folks?" I asked.

"Why upset them?"

In most families, I guess the next line would have been, "And don't you tell them, either." Among us kids, it wasn't necessary. Even though we squabbled, we never ratted on one another. Maybe being quints did give us some kind of bond.

* * *

There were days, and I guess even weeks, when we kind of forgot about being quintuplets. There are three girls and two boys, so that tells you right away we're not identical. Actually, if you ever saw the five of us together, you probably wouldn't guess we were even related.

Alice and Beth are most alike. They're both blond (getting blonder) and have greenish blue eyes. Craig's hair is a deeper (dirty) blond and he's a sturdy-looking guy. Drew is dark, with dark eyes like mine, and slimmer than Craig—"wiry" is what our parents call him. I'm thin myself, and the shortest of us all.

Natalie named us. She's our half-sister but she's lived in Colorado with her mom for years and years. She's out of college now and working in a radiology lab. Natalie was living with Dad and his wife Jean (that's our mom) when we were born, and she was the one who named us for the first five letters of the alphabet.

When anyone comments about my being the littlest, I always remember what Natalie used to whisper to me. "You're the littlest and the sweetest," she'd say. And I remember something else. She told me never to let anyone call me *quint*. "Your name is Emma," she said. "You just tell people that." Whenever I flew out to visit Natalie in Colorado, she always told her friends I was her little sister. My being a quintuplet was never mentioned. I'll bet most of her friends didn't even know there were five of us the very same age. Alice, Beth, Craig, and Drew visited Natalie once in a while, but not often and never together.

Our parents tried to play down the quint thing, too. At first, of course, they couldn't keep us out of the news. We were on TV when we were tiny babies and again on our first birthday. After that, no newspeople were allowed. The local media did sneak some shots when we started kindergarten, but then we moved to a different suburb.

We couldn't move too far away from the city because Dad and Mom both have jobs with the airlines. They put us in different schools, though . . . Alice, Craig, and Drew in one and Beth and me in another. Our parents met with the principals and asked that we be in separate classes as much as possible and that the teachers not mention we were quints. If Alice and Beth had been together, they'd have been thought of as twins. As it was, because Beth and I looked nothing alike, I guess kids just thought we had the same last name.

Our so-called fame was a thing of the past. Or so I thought. And I guess Beth had thought the same thing.

"What made that guy call now?" she asked Alice. "I mean, what's the big occasion?"

"He said because we're going to graduate from eighth grade."

"That's months away." Beth picked up a comb and whipped it through her hair. "We're only on spring break."

"He wants some backup, everyday shots, he said."

"How much did you tell him, anyway?" I asked, shifting to a cross-legged position. "And why did you talk to him at all? You know very well . . ."

"Don't get in a snit," Alice said. "I didn't tell him much of anything."

"You told him you were one of the quints."

"He asked. What was I supposed to tell him, that I was the upstairs parlormaid?"

"Look." Beth was leaning toward the mirror. "It's definitely blonder. Oh, I may have to wear a hat forever, until this grows out."

"That's clever," I said. "Absolutely everyone would notice you're a shade lighter, but no one would notice you were wearing a hat at the dinner table."

"Your turn," Beth said to Alice.

"I think I'll wait."

"No way! I'm not going to get chewed out alone!"

I got up and left the room. I knew how this was going to turn out. Within five minutes Alice would go and highlight her hair. The two of them always stuck together.

I went into my own private room. I'd have liked it better if I'd also had a private bath, but I had to share the connecting one with my sisters.

When we'd first moved to this house, all three of us were put in the same room. By the time I was seven, I begged Mom to let me move into the room reserved for Natalie's visits. Before saying I could, Mom made me write to Natalie to see how she felt about it.

Natalie didn't care. She was around eighteen by then. The next time she came for a visit, she said I should shove her stuff into a closet and fix up the room however I wanted. My big sister seemed to be more interested in seeing her old boyfriend, Noel, than in staring at a bunch of school stuff she'd left behind when she moved.

Just as I walked into my room the phone rang. I leaped and belly flopped onto the bed and snatched up the phone. "Princess Di here," I said. Just as the words leapt out of my mouth I thought, *Oh, no, what if it's that TV guy again?*

It was my friend, Gypsy.

"What's new at the palace?" she asked.

"Same boring routine . . . dashing about in the Rolls from one frightful charity bash to another."

"I say, that's bloody awful. Thought you might be out to the races. Or the polo grounds."

Gypsy and I can go on and on like this forever, but today I cut it short. "What did you find out about the classes?"

"They've already started, but they might take us in if we *qualify*."

"Meaning?"

"We'd have to audition."

"Uh. How do you audition?"

"Act out some speeches from a play, I guess," Gypsy said. "I dunno. We didn't go into that."

"Did you find out how much it costs?"

"No."

"Seems like you didn't find out a whole lot."

"The woman I talked to was busy, talking to about three other people at the same time. . . . You know how these acting studios are."

"No, I don't. How are they?"

"Like I said, busy. Anyway, she said we could stop by. I've got the address. Some Saturday morning, she said. I guess we'd better go tomorrow."

"Tomorrow? I'm too scared."

"You'd be just as scared a week from tomorrow. Besides, we've got to get started."

Gypsy and I agreed to meet the next day. Hanging up, I wondered how I'd gotten into this. At what point had I told Gypsy I wanted to be an actor someday? Or had I told her at all?

Gypsy's my newest and yet closest friend, but I have to admit she can be a little strange at times. Even her real name is a stretch. On the records it's Guinevere.

When I told Gypsy I'd never heard the name Guinevere outside of *Tales of King Arthur*, she said, "You've got it. Mom read those stories just before she dropped out of high school. I guess she was so proud of herself for getting through some actual literature, she had to let the world know."

"When did it get changed to Gypsy?" I asked.

"When I was about five, I saw the musical *Gypsy* on TV. I didn't understand the story but I loved the heroine's name."

"Didn't your mom object to the change?"

"No. Either she was sick of the name Guinevere or she could tell it didn't suit me."

At school, no matter what it said on the official records, Gypsy made it clear that she'd answer only to her own choice of name, even from the principal.

Someone gave five short raps on my door. It was the quint signal. Mom raps a couple of times. Dad usually just yells if he wants something.

"What?" I rolled off the bed and yanked open the door. It was Drew.

"What's coming off?" he asked. "What's the high-level conference all about?"

"Huh?"

"Alice just said we should all meet tonight. She wouldn't say why. Do you know?"

"Nope."

At that moment I didn't. After Drew had shrugged and left, it occurred to me that it might be about the reporter's phone call.

The five of us used to meet secretly late at night to talk over problems or to plan mischief. It was a long time since we'd done that. If Alice thought we should meet, it meant she had taken that phone call more seriously than she'd pretended. Did she actually think we'd agree to go public again as quints?

Give it up, Alice, I thought, *There's no way it's going to happen.* Beth might go along, but the boys wouldn't like the idea any more than I did. That would be three against two. And that wasn't even counting our parents!

CHAPTER 2

Dad didn't notice that his A and B daughters had become more blond. That wasn't surprising. Dad doesn't notice anything unless it personally inconveniences him. I'm not saying he's unfeeling. It's just that his work at the airline is pretty harrowing, so when he gets home he likes to relax. *He's shut down the control board* is what Craig always says when Dad acts like he's out of it.

Also—I hate to say this—Dad has an attitude about girls. I think it must date back to when he was a hotshot airline pilot and the stewardesses, as they used to call flight attendants, were handmaidens who had to follow orders.

Mom humors Dad most of the time, but when she does tell him off he deflates like punched-out bubble wrap.

"Where's Sylvester?" Dad suddenly asked when we were halfway through dinner. Syl's our Irish setter. "Don't tell me he had the decency to chase a car and die?"

"Dad!" Beth almost choked on a forkful of food. "You're awful!"

"He's at the vet's," Drew said. "Getting a pedicure."

Now it was Dad who almost choked. "Pedicure? For that mangy dog? Are you guys out of your minds?" He meant all of us. Dad likes to pretend we all ganged up against him about the dog. The truth is, Sylvester and Dad adore each other. It's often Dad who slips Syl a forbidden bite or two of people food.

Mom passed the mashed potatoes to Dad. "He's getting shots. If anyone in this family runs out for a pedicure, it's going to be me."

At this point Alice, who can't stand not to be noticed, piped up and asked, "Dad, what do you think of our hair?"

"What?" He looked up. "Whose hair?"

"Beth's and mine. Didn't you even notice?"

Dad looked puzzled for a moment, then said, "Is that the style now, all frizzed up?"

"Oh, really!" Alice rolled her eyes in exasperation. "We're blonder. Can't you tell?"

"Of course I noticed," Dad said, lying through his teeth. "I just didn't want to call attention to it and embarrass you."

"Sure," Alice said.

"But since you brought it up yourself," Dad said, now back at the controls, "you look like a couple of tarts."

"Jack . . ." Mom objected.

"What kind of tarts?" Craig wisecracked. "Apple? Cherry?"

"You looked like nice, normal little girls before," Dad went on, "so why do you have to go and freak yourselves up?"

"We're not *little girls*," Alice said. "We've reached puberty."

Dad hates that kind of talk. He'd like to think we're going to stay young forever. No matter how often we object, he always calls us *little girls*.

"What kind of plans do you all have for tomorrow?" Mom asked, getting up for the dessert. I was glad to see it was a lemon pie and not tarts of any kind.

Drew was going to hang out at his friend Fred's, Craig was planning to shoot baskets with some kids down the street, Alice and Beth were going to the mall with friends.

"And you, Emma?" Mom asked.

"Uh." I had to be evasive so I wouldn't be kidded if the acting class didn't happen. "Gypsy and I, uh . . . whatever." Without knowing it, Dad came to my rescue by urging Craig for about the millionth time to "hone his skills" so he'd make the basketball team in high school.

*   *   *

That evening, after I'd washed my hair and done some work on a school project, I lay on my bed reading and waiting for the secret quint rap on the door. By now Alice might have talked Beth into going public, but what approach would she make to the boys?

I jumped when the taps finally came late that night, and went along with the girls to our brothers' room.

Our house is old-fashioned-looking, and big. The rooms are high ceilinged and oversize compared to those in some of the houses our friends live in. And it's much bigger than our old house.

The whole second floor is just four bedrooms. Our parents have the huge one at the back of the house. My room's next, and then the girls'. Craig and Drew have the room at the front of the house, so we met there that evening, to be as far away from our parents as possible.

"All right, I'll be the one to ask," Craig started off. "Why are we gathered here together? To sing and pray?"

"To talk," Alice said.

"And to pray," I couldn't resist adding, "that the folks don't find out what we're here to talk about."

Craig whistled. "Sounds interesting . . . very interesting."

"It's about the quint thing," Alice said. She reached up and grabbed Drew's ankle as he was about to leave. "Come back here."

"Why? I'm not interested in 'the quint thing.'" He made it sound like something stupid.

"Suit yourself," Alice said, letting go of his ankle. "We'll decide without you."

"Come on, sit down," Craig said. "I'm not going to battle these babes alone." He put up his arms to ward off pillow slams from Beth.

Drew hesitated, then slumped back to the floor. "So speak."

"You don't get a doggy biscuit until you do, Alice," Craig said.

"You guys . . . !" Alice glared at each of us, heaved a big sigh, and said, "I should have just said we would, and then sat back to see how well you all handled it!"

"Could we just cut to the chase?" I asked. "What Alice is trying to say is that they want us to be on TV when we graduate."

"How do you know?" Craig asked her.

"Some guy called me." Alice tried to sound innocent. "They want the exclusive right to interview us beforehand and then film the ceremony."

"Who's *they?*"

"The local TV station. Not the network," Alice said. "This wouldn't be national news."

"Don't break my heart," Craig said. Then he added, "You're in trouble, you know."

"Me?" Alice was indignant. "All I did was answer the phone. This guy asked if I was one of the quintuplets. When I said yes, he gave me this bit about how everyone wanted to know more about us, and how we belonged to the world, like any celebrity . . ."

Drew muttered, "Oh, get a grip!" Craig gagged.

"Well, it's true!" Alice punched the pillow that was lying on her lap. Then she slammed it against Drew's chest.

"Maybe we had a kind of fame when we were born," I said. "That was news, I guess. But who cares about us now?"

"You'd be surprised," Beth said. "Not at school, maybe, but at other places people sometimes ask stuff like, do we have any siblings . . . and—"

"Right," Alice broke in. "So what are we supposed to tell them?"

"You don't have to tell them anything," Craig said to Beth.

Alice glared. "I'm not rude like you. All I say is that I have two sisters and two brothers, and nothing else unless they ask their ages."

"And then when we tell them," Beth said, "that we're all the same age, people think we're putting them on unless we explain that we're quintuplets."

"Do you believe these tarts?" Craig said to Drew. And then to Alice, "What's the point of our being in separate schools and separate activities if you're going to blow our cover?"

"I'm not ashamed to admit I'm a quint," Alice said. "Although I'd hate to have to identify you two as my brothers."

"Likewise."

"Could we get to the point?" I asked, trying to lift one of Craig's hand weights and almost cramping my arm muscle.

"The next time the guy calls, just say no, to coin a phrase," Craig said. "That's all. NO."

"What if he won't take no for an answer?"

"That's his problem."

"What if he starts stalking us? Taps our phones?"

"Alice, look at yourself in the mirror," Craig said. "Ask, 'Have I been watching too much late-night television? Am I losing it, here?' "

"I think we should tell the folks," I said. "Let Dad tell this guy off."

"Oh, great!" Alice said. "That would really get me in trouble!"

"It's not your fault you happened to answer the phone," I told her. "This one time."

Even in the fairly dim light I could see Alice flush. "Actually, I've talked to the guy a couple of times."

"You didn't tell me that!" Beth said.

"Well, I thought he'd give up. But he won't."

"You must have played along a little," Drew said, "Let him think we might go for it."

"Would that be so awful?" Alice got up angrily and plopped onto the edge of Drew's bed. "What's wrong with being a little bit famous? Lots of people wish they could be, and here we have the chance . . ."

"I, personally, don't want to be famous for being born," I said. "If I become well known I want it to be for something I've done."

"Good luck to that." Beth shrugged. "Anyway, I guess there's no point in even saying 'Maybe.' Mom and Dad would say 'No way.' "

"If we told them," Alice said.

"Oh, right." Craig took the weight from me and pumped it up and down, showing off. "Do you think they're not going to notice a bunch of TV cameras and lights in front of the house?"

"Baxter said we could film somewhere else, like the forest preserve."

We said it together. *"Baxter?"*

Alice flushed again, deeper this time. "He's the one who called."

"Well, aren't we friendly! Baxter!" Craig hooted.

"You guys are so . . . !" Alice got up and all but stepped on us as she stomped toward the door. "He asked my name and when I said Alice, he said he was Baxter. Make something of it!"

"Sounds like a dog name. Ark arf, come here boy. Here, Baxter!" Drew said.

Alice slammed out of the room. I hoped the noise wouldn't wake up our parents. They'd wonder why, all of a sudden, the five of us were in the same room, by choice.

"Why are you guys so mean to Alice?" Beth asked.

"We're not being mean," I said. "We just don't want to be exploited."

"Especially by anyone named"—and here the boys said it in unison—"*Baxter!*"

"It would only be one little TV feature," Beth pointed out. "Would that hurt so much?"

"Yes," the three of us said together.

"Remember Raymond, that kid who used to live down the block?" Craig asked. "Remember what he used to yell? 'Quinty, quinty, brains so splinty!'"

"That was a long time ago," Beth said. "Besides, I never got it."

"I did," Drew said. "He meant our brain was split five ways, so each of us just had one-fifth of a brain."

"That's stupid."

"Right, but I don't want that kind of attention ever again," Drew went on. "Kids get jealous. They think you're showing off and they get even."

"Oh, grow up." Beth got up and left the room, too.

17

The boys and I waited a moment. Then Drew said, "What'll we do about Alice?"

"Let her fantasize, the twit. She'll give it up," Craig said, lowering the weight to the floor. "She knows what would happen."

"Right," Drew said, but he didn't sound so sure.

When I got back to my room I felt jittery. I knew Alice wouldn't just drop this idea. Underneath, she's always been a little proud of our infant fame. If she could get us back into the spotlight without the folks finding out until later, she'd go for it. Well, she could convince Beth, but not me and not the boys.

I'd meant it when I said I'd rather be famous for what I did. But I was glad I hadn't said, *Like being an actor.* Even my brothers would have broken up over that.

Thinking about the audition tomorrow made me jittery again. Was I kidding myself, even thinking I could act? I wished I had Gypsy's self-confidence. She didn't doubt herself . . . ever.

CHAPTER 3

I rode my bike over to Gypsy's. She lives on the outskirts of town in what I guess you'd have to call a run-down area. Most of the houses scream for a coat of paint and a yard cleanup. There are beat-up cars littering driveways and sometimes a bunch of tires and broken-down appliances on the front porches or in the yards.

Kurt was outside hammering on the front steps.

"Yo," he greeted me.

"Yo, Kurt," I replied. It was okay for me to use his first name because he wasn't Gypsy's father. He wasn't even her mom's husband, but he lived with them.

"No moving job today?" I asked. Kurt has a truck he uses as a moving van whenever he gets the chance.

"Not today. Tomorrow. Want to help?"

"Is Gypsy going to?"

"Yep." He marked across a long board with a pencil and then picked up a saw.

"Then maybe I will."

Just as I was wondering if I should step across the

open space where he was going to put the new step, Gypsy came out.

"Thought I heard you," she said. "Are you still nervous?"

"Yes, a little."

"You guys want a lift somewhere?" Kurt asked, holding the saw halfway through the board. Kurt has the attitude that work can always wait.

"No, we'll bike it," Gypsy said.

"Who's looking after the kids?" Kurt asked.

"You are," Gypsy answered, lifting her bike. "Until I get back." Usually Gypsy was stuck with her little sisters on weekends when her mother, Donnette, worked in a lingerie shop at the mall.

"Are they up?" Kurt asked.

"Yeah. Raven's eating breakfast and Sasha's watching TV. See you!"

Gypsy whirled away on her bike and I followed.

Somehow I'd assumed the acting studio was at the park field house, I don't know why. Maybe because so many activities for kids and grownups took place there. But Gypsy biked toward the downtown area.

"What did your family say about the acting classes?" she asked.

"Mom's the only one who knows. I broke the glad tidings to her this morning."

"Oh? And what did she say?"

"She thought it was a good idea. Mom's always very supportive."

Suddenly Gypsy braked in front of a laundromat.

"Why are you stopping?" I asked.

"We're here." She pulled out her lock and fastened her bike to a lamp post.

I looked around. "I don't see any . . ."

"What did you expect? Mann's Chinese Theatre . . . with the stars' handprints in cement?"

"Hardly, since that's in Hollywood." I'd seen the famous sidewalk on a trip to Los Angeles, when our family went to Disneyland. For that matter, I'd been on the Universal Studios trip, too.

That whole vacation package had been offered to our family when we, the quints, were five years old. The big catch was, the company would get to do a filmed account of our trip. Our folks refused, of course. When we were ten, though, they took us themselves. It wasn't that big a financial deal because both Mom and Dad get all kinds of air fare perks from their jobs.

After locking up my bike to the next lamp post, I followed Gypsy into the laundromat.

"If you'd told me, I could have brought along my muddy jeans and sneakers," I commented.

Gypsy opened a door at the back of the laundromat, and we went into a room with mirrors lining two walls and a barre for ballet. There were two girls of about seven sitting on the floor, tying on regular shoes. A mother beckoned to them and they left.

I raised my eyebrows at Gypsy, meaning, *What gives?*

She looked at her Swatch. "We're ten minutes early."

As I was beginning to think *Thank goodness, I don't have to do this,* a woman bustled in, carrying a huge patchwork pouch and an equally big overstuffed purse. If this was the drama instructor, I was taking a hike.

"Hi. I'm Helen. You ladies here for acting class?" she asked, opening her pouch and spewing stuff onto a table.

"No," I said.

"Yes," Gypsy said at the same instant.

"And you are . . . ?"

"Gypsy Callahan. I talked to you about coming. And this is my friend, Emma Wentworth, who's also interested in acting."

The woman dug through the pile of clutter. Finally she found a small notebook and flipped it open. "Mmmmm . . . oh, yes. Here are your names. You'll have to audition. But not now. After class. You can stay and observe."

She began greeting the kids who were coming into the room now. "Got that inflection down, Terri? . . . Find some motivation, Henry?"

I glanced at Gypsy, wondering if she was thinking the same thing I was. This woman was not my idea of what a drama coach should look like. I hadn't expected Meryl Streep, but still our instructor was a shock . . . overweight, stringy hair pulled back with a rubber band, not a trace of make-up.

"Does Helen have any credentials?" I whispered to Gypsy.

"Are you kidding? She's played summer stock back East and she's even been in some soaps."

"You're putting me on."

"Hey, Emma, looks aren't everything. Besides, lots

of plays and movies need regular-looking people to play some of the parts."

A girl called out, "Helen, you're gonna kill me, I didn't get it all memorized." She looked faintly familiar.

"I won't kill, just perhaps pulverize," the woman cheerfully answered.

"By sitting on her," I muttered.

"Emma, don't get an attitude," Gypsy said. "Try to keep open."

"I really don't want to be here."

"Yes, you do."

After watching about eight kids come in—and I have to say they all looked enthusiastic—I said to Gypsy, "These guys are all younger than we are."

"What's-her-name over there isn't. Cindy . . . Cathy . . . I've seen her at school."

"Corliss."

"Yeah . . . and here comes Dolores. You know Dolores."

"Right. What's she doing here?" I had recognized Dolores, a thin, pallid girl with the personality of a paper clip.

"Maybe she's trying to find herself," Gypsy said.

"There's no one there to find."

"Emma, you're being such a witch."

I was, I knew. Maybe it was because I had gone from being almost stiff with fear to being disgusted within a matter of minutes. I just couldn't picture this Helen person as my guide on the yellow brick road to fame and fortune. Or even as someone who knew all that much about acting.

If Gypsy and I had been seated near the door I might actually have slunk out. But we'd cleverly placed ourselves on folding chairs in the far corner.

Then Helen began to speak, and the air around her seemed to crackle with sheer energy. "I know you all saw the movie I assigned last week," she said. "And did you watch for Jake's reaction in the scene I warned you about? Where he suddenly realizes he's there alone?" She beamed with sheer delight at the class. "How did he show his feelings?"

The kids all yelled out. They were so into this!

"One at a time, please," Helen said with a laugh. "Dolores?"

And the girl I'd always thought of as a big zero actually started looking alive and involved as she described how the guy's smile faded, and then he looked puzzled and then seemed to hold his breath. She went on to tell how, with no movement of his body, just by facial expression, he let the audience know the realization had come over him . . . he was alone and in danger.

Then Helen assigned dramatic situations to pairs of kids and told them to work out how they'd show, without speech, what was going on. I couldn't see all their faces as they performed, but the ones I could see were really good.

It seemed as though only about twenty minutes had passed when Helen said, "Okay, thespians, time's up."

The class didn't seem to want to leave.

"Shoo!" Helen said. "Go home and work on your pantomimes. See you next week. And see some more movies in the meantime."

"Are you kidding?" Henry asked.

"No, I'm not kidding. I want you to focus on an individual actor. See what he or she does to make the role convincing. Observe, imitate, then create. That goes for most of the arts."

Wow. Imagine an assignment to watch movies! I could see myself getting out of chores around the house with the excuse, "I have to go down to Video Blowout to rent some flicks. It's not fun. It's homework." Yeah, in my dreams.

"You two," Helen called out as she shuffled stuff back into the patchwork pouch. "Come here and do your auditions."

My heart began racing.

"What do you have for me?" the teacher asked as we stood before her. "A speech from a play, what?"

"We didn't actually prepare anything," Gypsy said.

"Okay." This woman was nothing if not amiable. Even her voice had a nice gurgling sound. "Do a pantomime. What's your name again?"

"Gypsy."

"And you?"

"Emma Wentworth."

Helen wrinkled her forehead in a frown, though the rest of her face was still smiling. I'd already noticed she smiled a lot. "Wentworth . . ." she said. "Now why does that name seem familiar?"

I hoped I had enough acting ability to look as though I couldn't imagine why my name should seem familiar.

Her frown lines vanished. "I know. Wentworth was the name of my favorite Sunday school teacher."

"That must have been ages ago," Gypsy said. What a diplomat.

"Centuries," Helen agreed. "Okay, you, Emma. I want you to take an ice cream bar out of the freezer and eat it."

"Huh?"

"Pantomime," Gypsy murmured.

"Yes, pantomime," Helen said, sitting on one of the folding chairs. She beamed another big smile at me.

For a couple of seconds I felt paralyzed. Then I thought of our freezer at home. It was at the bottom instead of the top of the refrigerator.

I stooped down and pulled on an imaginary handle and swung out an imaginary door. I pretended to shuffle through packages. Then I located them! Ha! With a gleam of pleasure, I took out the carton, opened it, and took out a bar. Then I put the rest of them back, closed the door, and began eating. I thought it was pretty neat the way I took a pretend bite, wiped my lip where the chocolate had smudged, and kept on eating until only the stick remained, which I tossed into a garbage can. I licked a pretend drop off my finger. The End!

"Very good," Helen said. "You really got into it. I especially liked it when you licked off the drips. You just can't eat an ice cream bar without dripping. And you really seemed to be enjoying it."

"I didn't get the flavor," Gypsy said.

I gave her a withering look.

Helen laughed. "Criticism, both deserved and undeserved, is all a part of acting. When you get up and perform, you're opening yourself to comments. Anyone who wants to act has to learn to listen when it's helpful and to ignore destructive remarks. And build up a thick hide."

I wasn't sure I could.

"There's only one thing you forgot in the pantomime," Helen went on. "You forgot to remove the wrapping."

I started to protest . . . but bars do come in wrappings inside the package. "You're right," I said. "I just forgot."

"In pantomime it's very important to concentrate on every action. Forget your audience. Forget everything except what you're doing at the moment."

She turned to Gypsy. "I want you to pour coffee and do everything connected with that, and then after you've drunk a little, you realize something's very wrong with it. Ready?"

Gypsy closed her eyes, thought for a moment, and then said, "Okay."

She poured coffee, set down the pot, reached over and put sugar into the cup and then cream, and stirred. Then she lifted the cup to her lips, suddenly crossed her eyes, clutched her throat with her free hand, and dropped the cup. I was wondering if she was going to fall on the floor in the throes of death, but thank goodness she stopped short of that.

"I can see you have a dramatic flair," Helen said when Gypsy had finished. "You did everything as you should have except you skipped one thing. Know what that is, Emma?"

I shook my head no. I couldn't think of anything Gypsy had left out, though, in my opinion, there were a couple of things she should have.

"You didn't swallow," Helen said.

Gypsy's eyes widened. "I didn't?"

The teacher laughed. "You're not alone. You'd be surprised how many actors' throats don't move when they're supposed to be drinking."

She stood up. "See you girls next week," she said. "Prepare another pantomime. It's lucky you've only missed one class before this one." She opened the door and we followed her. "Oh, and I guess you'd better bring a check or cash next week." She fished a couple of orange papers from her pouch and handed them to us. "Here's all the information."

As we trudged through the laundromat on our way out, Helen suddenly stopped and said, "I almost forgot my stuff!"

As we left, she was pulling clothes out of a dryer and tossing them into a yellow plastic basket.

Outside, Gypsy said, "In spite of her looks, she's pretty sharp. Right?"

"Right." Unlocking my bike, I said, "I held my breath when she wondered about my name."

"How come?"

I snapped a look at Gypsy. "Because . . ." I didn't know how to say it without sounding self-important. "Some people still remember the . . . well . . . fuss made over us when we were born. I told you about it." Gypsy was the only one I'd told. Maybe I'd made a mistake even telling *her*.

"You mean being quintuplets? Come on, that's history."

"But we still *are*, you know."

"Sure, but nobody cares."

That stung just a little. I thought of telling Gypsy about the TV reporter and how he wanted to do a feature on us. I didn't, though. Wasn't it my wish that people would forget all about my wondrously weird birth?

CHAPTER 4

*W*hen I got home Mom was out picking up Sylvester at the vet's. She'd left a note. No one else was around. I knew Mom hadn't taken my four brothers and sisters because (a) they wouldn't have wanted to go, and (b) we almost never went anywhere in a bunch.

Long ago, my parents had learned that taking all five babies somewhere was asking for a mob scene. They might take two . . . never dressed like twins, and never more than two. This rule made for some complications. There always had to be a sitter. Most of the time we had a full-time housekeeper who would baby-sit. My parents tried to be very fair and take along different kids in a sort of sequence. If they took two of us, it was seldom Alice and Beth together, because they looked so much alike. They could take me—smaller and darker —with one of the other girls, or with a brother. Once in a while they took the two boys together because Craig and Drew were so different.

I know it all sounds strange and complicated, but to

us kids it was just the normal way of life. On the rare occasions when we all went to the movies, we'd split up . . . two with one parent and three with the other. And we never went into the theater together.

In a way it got simpler as we grew older. If we took a couple of friends along, it looked like a birthday celebration and people tended to steer clear of groups like that. It helped, too, that now we could go off on our own. We didn't need our parents to haul us around all the time.

My pantomime had given me huge longings for a real ice cream bar. I was shoving stuff around in the freezer drawer when the kitchen door opened and the massive dog-creature came roaring in.

"Oh, Sylvester, calm down," Mom said. "You weren't away that long."

"So, mutt," I said, digging my hands into the fur around his collar. "Did the doc give you a lollipop?"

"He was so pathetically glad to see me," Mom said. "He dribbled some, but luckily we were out on the street by then."

"Why'd he have to stay overnight just for shots?"

"Because I couldn't pick him up yesterday evening. Where is everyone?"

"I don't know. I just got here."

"How was your class?" Mom got a bottle of club soda from the refrigerator. "Was it fun?"

"We just observed. Oh, and I had to pantomime eating an ice cream bar. I was hoping to find a real one just now."

"Behind the bags of vegetables."

I moved some stuff around, and sure enough . . . victory!

As I pulled off the paper, I had to laugh. "In my pantomime, I forget to remove the wrapper."

Mom smiled. I sat down at the kitchen table opposite her.

"Did you ever think of being an actor?" I asked.

"Not seriously. I acted in a few plays, though."

"Really?" This was news. "When?"

"In high school. And then in college. Once I played Ophelia in *Hamlet*."

"What? You're kidding! I never knew that!"

Mom took a swallow of water and set down the glass. "It was a long time ago. Fun. Very exciting." She looked amused. I guess I was sitting there with my mouth open. "Emma, why should you be surprised?" And then, kidding, "Didn't you imagine I had a life before all you kids?"

"Yes, but . . ." I was thinking, *Maybe acting is in my blood!* "You never talk about it. Don't you miss your stage life?"

Mom laughed. "It wasn't a life, Emma. It was just something I did back then. I hardly ever even think about it."

"Would you like it if I became an actor?"

"Honey, I would like for you to do whatever you want to do."

This seemed a good moment to ask. "I don't have enough money for the lessons. Unless you let me withdraw some from my savings account."

"How much?"

I told her.

"That doesn't sound drastic. I think we can bankroll you."

"Really?"

Mom got up and put her empty glass in the dishwasher. "I keep track of little extras . . . sports equipment, special events, gifts. You never ask for much. It's your turn."

"Oh, Mom." I got up and put my arms around her. "You're so nice." *Nice* was a pale kind of word, but she knew I meant more.

"There's just one thing . . ." Mom said.

"What?"

"I expect front row seats to your opening night on Broadway."

It felt so good to be the only one there with Mom. It happened once in a while, but not very often. I wondered how it would feel to be an only child. Good, I bet.

My half-sister Natalie had been an only child for years and years. And then wha-bam! She got blasted with five brothers and sisters at once. It's a wonder she didn't come unhinged.

* * *

Sunday, after lunch, I started to leave the house.

"Now where are you off to?" Dad asked. "Do you kids always have to be running off somewhere?"

"I'm going to Gypsy's."

"To do what?"

Dad should have been a prosecuting attorney.

33

"To . . . well, actually, to help her . . . to help Kurt . . . move some people."

"What?"

"He's a mover. Part time."

"I know he's a part-time mover and a full-time nothing. But what does this moving have to do with you? What do you do, help him haul grand pianos around?"

"Dad, Gypsy and I just log in the boxes. We make a list of what goes into the truck and what comes out of it. To see that nothing gets lost on the way."

"And this tracking of boxes . . . this is your idea of a profitable way to spend time, especially on Sunday?" Once he got started, Dad didn't let up. "By the way, where are your sisters?"

"They went with Mom to visit Aunt Toots. Because you wouldn't go."

"Oh." Dad picked up the paper, hoping, I guess, that I'd say no more.

Drew came rushing into the room. "Hey, Pop. They're having a big sale on camping equipment at that new place by the mall. Ted's dad's taking us and I thought you might want to go along."

"Why would you think that?" Dad asked.

As they were arguing about the fun of camping (according to Drew) versus the fact that it was a pain in the neck (according to Dad), I took off.

On my way over to Gypsy's I wondered if the girls would tell Mom about the TV feature idea on the drive to Aunt Toots's house. They might tell her, I thought, to try to get her to convince Dad. But then I thought,

No, they won't. While Mom's often on our side, when it comes to publicity she and Dad form a united front.

I was pretty sure Alice wouldn't tell Mom. But what would she do? I didn't have a clue.

* * *

I got to Gypsy's just in time to ride along with her and Kurt to the house where they were doing the moving job. Actually, it wasn't a whole houseful of stuff, just what belonged to a couple of roommates who were moving out from other roommates for reasons unknown to Gypsy and me.

Gypsy set up her rickety bridge table and folding chairs and made a list of the things that were being shoved into the back of the truck. It was such junk. The guys' sofa was all faded and had sagging springs. Their TV had glass rings on the top. Their dishes were so disgusting looking I wouldn't have used them for Sylvester's food. I couldn't see it mattered if any of it was lost in transit.

"That's not the point," Gypsy said when I expressed my opinion. "This is good training for me."

"For doing what?"

"For studying people. You meet all kinds in the moving business. Some good, some bad, some ugly. If you notice, I talk to all types. For acting, you can take a characteristic from just about anyone and build on it."

I wondered where Gypsy had gotten all this insight. Not from her mother, whose idea of deep thinking is deciding what shade of eye shadow to wear. And certainly not from Kurt. "You're that serious about acting?" I asked.

"Sure. Aren't you?"

"I guess so."

At that point Gypsy switched the conversation back to work. "I'm going to start marking some of these mystery boxes," she said, picking up a fat marking pen. "I'll call out the number and what's in the box, and you can write it down."

When the truck was loaded, we drove to the guys' new place and did everything in reverse. Mostly they hauled belongings out of the truck before Gypsy could even see what they were and call over to me, but we did the best we could. Nothing seemed to be lost or damaged.

A sudden racket made me jump. I turned and looked toward the street. There were three boys coming along, two on skateboards and one on Rollerblades. They glanced at us, then one yelled something to the others. They all stopped and went to the top of the driveway across the street. It was higher than the one where our truck was parked. The boys lined up and then came clacking down, whirling right across the street and into our driveway.

CHAPTER 5

*T*he noise stopped as the boys stopped. One of them was tall, one medium, and one on the short side.

"Well, well, the Three Stooges," Gypsy said, wandering toward the boys. I stayed behind.

She started talking to them, mostly to the one who was about her height once he was off the skateboard. His hair was just a little spiked and he was wearing a wild shirt that went down almost to the bottom of his shorts. The tallest one, the one on Rollerblades, was wearing ordinary jeans and a T-shirt, and stayed a little to the side.

Gypsy turned and motioned to me to join them.

I didn't want to go. I get really embarrassed meeting new people, particularly boys. But I couldn't think of any way to escape. Gypsy turned toward me once again, and I finally walked over.

"Emma," she said, "these daredevils on wheels are dying to meet you, especially the tall one."

I don't know who blushed more, him or me.

"What's your name again, Jim?"

"James."

"Oh. James, Emma. Emma, James."

We each managed a "Hi." Then we both looked away.

"And this is Wharton . . . you sure you're not putting me on?" Gypsy asked.

"It used to be Warthog but we shortened it. Hi, Emma. And this is Billy." Wharton gestured toward the short kid.

Billy, broken up over the Warthog thing, managed a snickering "Hi."

"They live just down the street," Gypsy told me. "They go to Hudson School."

"That's nice." I didn't know what else to say.

"No, it's not. The school stinks," Wharton said. "You guys are lucky to go to Stevenson. Want to trade off? Trade identities?"

"Sure," Gypsy said. She was so calm you'd think these were old-time buddies. "I'll say one thing. Your school has a killer basketball team."

I knew for a fact Gypsy couldn't care less about sports. But she knew how to talk to boys.

"You ought to come over to our games," Wharton said. "See some experts in action. See how the game is played."

"Basketball season's over," James said.

I decided to jump in. "Do you play?" I asked Wharton.

"Nope. He does." He cocked a thumb at James.

"Oh. So does my brother." I didn't mention that both

of my brothers and one of my sisters went to James's school.

"So what do you do if you're not playing on the team?" Gypsy asked Wharton. Her voice had taken on a subtly husky tone.

"I hang around pretty girls."

Kurt saved me, at least, from further stupid chatter. "Hey," he called out, "are you about ready to roll?" Then he headed toward the house with some papers for the guys to sign.

The boys looked slightly startled, but Gypsy called back, "Just a minute, Kurt."

"He's ready to go," I said, starting toward the truck. I paused, called out "Nice to meet you" to the boys, and walked on.

Gypsy dashed back to the card table, tore off a piece of paper, and rushed back to the boys. When she returned, she was shoving the paper into her pocket. "I got their numbers," she said to me.

"Their what?"

"Telephone numbers. The best policy is to get theirs, then it's your decision."

"What is?"

She gave me an I-don't-believe-you look. "Whether to call them or not. Don't tell me you give out your number."

"Of course not."

"Well, then." She waved as the boys took off down the street.

I hesitated for a moment. "Gypsy . . . you didn't . . . ?"

39

"What?"

"Tell them—" I felt a little silly saying it—"that I'm a quint?"

Gypsy stared at me. "Why would I tell them a dumb thing like that?"

I shrugged. "Some kids would, if they knew."

"Well, I wouldn't. I know how you hate it. Have I ever told anyone at school?"

"No." I felt sure she hadn't.

"Well, I'm not about to start blabbing it around to boys. It's tough enough keeping them interested in me!"

After Gypsy and I'd got the table and other stuff into the truck, we pulled ourselves up to the front seat. "So which one do you want?" Gypsy asked. "I think the tall one would probably be the best for you."

This was a side of Gypsy I'd never seen before. Of course I hadn't known her all that long.

Before I could think of an answer Kurt came out of the house, stuffing money into his jeans pocket. When he got into the driver's seat, he wriggled, pulled out the bills again, and handed a few to Gypsy. "You girls can divvy it up any way you want to."

I refused my share. I knew Gypsy didn't get an allowance. She got sister-sitting money from her mom, but she told me she'd be using all she'd saved for the acting classes.

"What did you think of them?" she asked Kurt.

"Who, those young studs? I didn't really check them out."

"I suspect they're kind of simpleminded when you

40

get to know them, but they should make good practice material," Gypsy said.

"In what way?" Kurt steered with one hand as he reached over to the cigarette lighter and lit up a cigarette.

"For flirting."

Kurt laughed just as he inhaled, which made him choke a little. "So that's how you gals do it. Practice on the losers."

"I didn't say Wharton was a loser. Just probably not very bright."

"Well, Gyp, do like your mother does and you'll be all right," Kurt said.

"Oh, spare me," Gypsy answered.

It seemed to me that Gypsy was a lot smarter than her mother could ever be, and she certainly had more ambition. But I hoped she wasn't going to be like her mom when it came to hanging out with guys.

And then I happened to think . . . maybe Gypsy wasn't out to pick up a guy. She was just doing what she'd talked about before. Trying to meet new people so she could study some of their characteristics. For acting. That could be it. *Yeah, sure it could.*

Get real, I thought. Gypsy had been picking up Wharton. So? Kids did it all the time. And wouldn't it be fun and exciting for me to work up a telephone friendship with James? Laugh and talk the way Alice and Beth did with boys from their classes? Only I wouldn't carry on like some addle-brained twit, the way my sisters sometimes did. And James, though he'd be lighthearted and fun to talk to, would be serious at times, too.

After we'd known each other for a year or two he and I might even go out on dates. (Even in a daydream I couldn't produce a scenario where Dad would let me date any sooner.) And through the years James and I would have these great conversations and understandings, so even if our paths went in different directions, we'd always keep in touch and be friends.

I realized Gypsy was looking at me.

"What?" I asked.

"I said, do you have to go home right away? If not, we could call the guys . . . just to rattle their cages."

Kurt laughed again.

"I have to get home," I said, more tightly than I meant to.

"Okay. It was just a thought."

When we got to Gypsy's, I headed for my bike.

"Here, take this." She reached into her pocket.

"Really, I don't want any money."

"I wasn't going to offer *that* again." Gypsy pulled out the slip with the numbers on it and tore off the bottom one. "This is James's. Call him. What can you lose?"

I shrugged and stuck the paper into my jeans pocket.

What could I lose? My dignity, for one thing. I'd never call up a guy I'd just met.

Besides, what if he thought I was a zero, a negative number? And he brushed me off? I'd never risk that. Never.

CHAPTER 6

*A*s I was about to go into my room, Mom came down the hall. "Oh, honey, you had a phone call," she said.

"I did?" I was glad of the gloom out there in the hall, because I could feel my face flushing.

"Yes, just a little while ago. I wasn't sure when you'd be back."

Gypsy had called him and told him to call me. No, she didn't have his number. It was in my pocket. She'd called Wharton and told him to tell James to call me. I wasn't ready for this.

"Emma? Are you all right?" Mom asked.

"Uh . . . yeah. Why?"

"You seem a little . . . I don't know."

"I'm okay."

"Well, anyway, she's going out, so she said she couldn't call back. I guess what she had to tell you will keep."

Oh. A she. "This was . . . Gypsy?"

"No, honey. Natalie."

"Natalie! Oh, Mom!" Every other concern faded away as I thought about my big sister. I loved her so much and just lived for my visits with her. There were times when, if it weren't for Mom, I'd want to move out to Colorado Springs and live with Natalie. "Did you talk to her?"

"Yes, for a while. She loves her job, and she's moved into her own apartment. She can see Pike's Peak from her front window."

"If spring break weren't over, I'd go out there."

"Mmmm." Mom went downstairs and I went into my room.

I found myself thinking for some reason about Natalie and Dad. They didn't get along too well. "He's so bossy, so bull-headed" was how she described him.

"Was that why you moved out, when we were still little?" I once asked her.

"Partly that. He treated me like a live-in baby-sitter. But then I left partly to get away from being called 'sister of the quints.' When you guys came along, I almost lost my identity."

"Sorry."

"Come on, it wasn't your fault. If it had been you alone, instead of that five-pack, it would have been okay." Natalie had paused then. "But I guess I moved away mostly because I needed my own mother, and she needed me."

"Yeah. Your mother's nice."

"Well, so is Jean. I got along with her fine. She even stood up for me when Dad got really obnoxious."

"She does for us, too," I had told Natalie. "But it seems to me Dad is chilling out a little."

"I guess it's hard for him to ride herd on five of you. When I was the age you are now, there was just me." Natalie had looked thoughtful. "And then, poor Dad's not as young as he used to be."

I had felt a tiny squeeze in my chest. "He's not old!"

"Not *old* old. But he's not the young lion he used to be."

I didn't say anything, but I must have looked just a little upset because Natalie had given my hair a playful yank and said, "Cheer up. He's still got the energy to bark out orders and try to run your life. That'll never change."

She was so right.

* * *

School started again the next day, and the only good thing was that we were now in the final stretch before eighth grade graduation. Kids were already talking about summer plans.

Gypsy met me at my locker and we walked along to homeroom.

"Did you call him?" she asked. She'd done her hair in a different way. Instead of just letting it hang down past her shoulders, she'd whipped up part of it and let it waterfall down from a clip. It made her look older. "Oh, you don't even have to answer," she said. "I know you. You need a shove."

"So how many times did you call Wharton?"

"Just once. He called me the other times."

"Which would add up to?"

"Four or five."

I mentally adjusted that to two or three. Gypsy has a way of exaggerating.

"What did you find to talk about?"

"Everything."

"I wouldn't know how to start," I said.

"There ought to be courses for girls like you, Emma. Boy-Girl Conversation 101. How to Pick Up a Guy and Make Him Think He Picked You Up 102. How to Fast-Forward Relationships 103."

"Yeah, yeah."

We were at our homeroom now. As I went to my assigned seat, I couldn't help wishing there were such courses. I'd burn rubber getting there to sign up. Of course, by just hanging around Gypsy I'd learn a lot, too. Her methods weren't the kind Miss Manners would recommend, but I could observe and adapt. Four or five phone calls. Or two or three. Impressive either way.

That night after about an hour of homework—the teachers were loading it on—I finally got up the courage to call James. I mean, what could I lose? He didn't know me. I didn't know anyone who knew him. No danger to my pure, pure rep.

I went to the bathroom I shared with Alice and Beth to get the phone. It wasn't there. When our folks finally broke down and let us have our own line, they said we had to share. There was an extra long cord on the Princess phone (Dad said it was well named, in our case) so we could take it into either room.

I went out to the hall and into their room.

Instead of lying sprawled on the bed, Alice was sitting on the side of the bed as she talked on the phone. When she saw me, she said, "Just a minute, please," and to me, "What do you want?"

"The phone."

"All right, just a minute. I'll knock on your door."

I nearly fainted. This was a new, gentler Alice. It made me suspicious.

She stared at me, waiting. I shrugged and left.

A minute later I was sitting at my desk. Beth came to my door and then on inside my room.

"What's up?"

"I have a feeling Alice is talking to that guy again. Baxter. She asked me not to come in just now."

I'd forgotten about the TV show. "What should we do? Tell the folks?"

"That's easy for you to say. You don't share a room with Alice."

"Yeah." I thought for a minute. "Let's alert the boys. They can let her know that if she sets up an interview, she'll be the only one there."

"Good idea. You tell them."

I looked at Beth. She was never going to be an assertive woman, at least not around Alice. But, as she said, she had to room with her.

The bathroom door opened and Alice came in with the phone. She looked at us a bit warily. "What's going on?"

"You kicked me out of the room," Beth said. "So what did you want?"

"Oh, that. Well, it was personal. Here's the phone, Emma. Don't hog it all night."

They left, and I glanced at the phone. Suddenly it looked lethal. It could be the weapon that transformed me into a boy-chaser.

It rang. I gave a little shriek.

The call was probably for one of my sisters.

"Hello," I said hesitantly.

It was a boy's voice on the other end, clearing its throat. "Is this Emma?"

"Yes."

"This is James."

Oh, my God. I couldn't utter a sound.

"Do you remember me? We were the guys . . ."

He sounded as scared as I felt. That gave me a touch of courage. I even managed to sound offhand when I said, "Oh, yes, at the moving place." *Moving place. Brilliant.*

"That's right. I was the one on Rollerblades."

"I remember." *Tall, curly hair. Cute!*

"So how have you been?"

Since two days ago? This was not brilliant, either, but hey, we both seemed to be interns at this. "Good," I said. "I started back to school today." *What a hot flash. So did two thousand other kids.*

"Yeah, so did I. It's a drag."

"Right. A drag."

"So are you doing homework?"

"Sort of."

"Me, too. Oh . . . I guess my mom wants to use the phone. So long. See you."

"See you."

Well. It hadn't been much of a conversation, but at least it was a beginning. And he'd called *me!* I was dying to let Gypsy know, and even reached for the phone, but then I thought I'd wait and just mention it casually sometime. That is, if James ever called again. If he didn't, it was better not to get Gypsy started asking, "What do you hear from James?"

In my mind, I went over what he and I had said. Weak. I'd try to do better next time. If there was a next time.

CHAPTER 7

I tried to phone Natalie several times that week, but all I got was her answering machine. What had she wanted to tell me? Was it about moving to her new place? I hoped it was something more romantic than that.

I didn't hear from James again. He must have thought I was really dim. Or maybe he thought he'd been. Should I call him? I couldn't decide.

On Saturday Gypsy and I went to acting class again.

Helen was wearing a plaid top that fought with her patchwork pouch, and she had her hair pulled back with a rubber band the same as the week before. She looked like someone out to do laundry, which she probably was.

"Girls!" she greeted us. "I'm so glad you came back for more. Some don't."

"We can take criticism," Gypsy said. "Oh, here's my money." She handed over some wadded bills and I gave Helen my check.

"Criticism, as long as it's constructive, is the best thing for you at this stage," Helen said as she shoved the money and check into her purse. "It'll toughen you up for the auditions."

"Auditions for what?" The kid named Henry had joined us.

"You'll find out in good time," Helen said, beaming.

I wondered what she meant.

After the whole class had gathered, Helen said she'd pair each of us with a partner and told us we were going to do improvs . . . improvisations. "I'll name a situation and then you guys jump in."

Helen moved her folding chair next to ours so she could be part of the audience. "The first one is this, Dolores and Corliss. One of you has invited the other to a movie. But just before you get there you realize you don't have any money with you. Go!"

I shrank in my seat as I realized I wouldn't have had the faintest idea how to proceed. I wondered if they knew.

To my great surprise, the two girls walked to the front of the room, whispered a moment, then acted as though they were walking down the street.

"Oh, gee," Corliss said, suddenly jamming her fingers against her mouth, looking embarrassed. "Maybe we shouldn't see this movie after all. I just remembered. I read a review that said it stunk."

"Really? I read a review that said it's terrific!" Dolores answered. She sounded and looked so sure of herself. Could this be the no-personality Dolores I knew, sort of?

"You'd probably rather see it with your parents," Corliss said. Her eyes looked this way and that.

"Why?"

"Well . . ." Corliss hesitated. "It's R-rated!"

"No, it's not."

"It's a really long movie," Corliss said, now biting her lips. "Really long."

"We've got all afternoon," Dolores replied.

It went on like this until Helen, checking a stopwatch, said, "Time!"

The girls went back to their seats.

"That was pretty good," Helen said. "Corliss, I liked the way you let us know you were embarrassed but tried to hide it from Dolores. Dolores, I liked your breezy attitude and comebacks."

Personally, I thought they'd both been terrific. And now I fervently wished I could fade from this scene before I had to get up there and show off my ignorance. Who would be next?

"Gypsy?" Helen looked up from her list. "By the way, you might want to rethink that name if you go pro."

"Why?" Gypsy asked.

"It sounds like a stripper. There was one once, you know—Gypsy Rose Lee."

As the kids laughed, Gypsy said, "I'll change the image."

"There you go. Now let's get on with the improv. You and Henry are in this situation: You've, quote, borrowed your father's car, Henry, and have dented the fender. You don't want your girl to know how scared you are."

Gypsy and Henry did the improv and it was okay, I guess, but I didn't really focus on it. I was mostly sitting there shaking, knowing my turn was coming.

After Helen commented favorably on their acting, she turned to me as I knew she would. But I wasn't prepared for what she had to say.

"Emma, I realized after class last time why your name sounded familiar. You're one of the Wentworth quints, aren't you?"

I felt as though I was melting down. I wished I could. "Quints?" I stammered.

She frowned. "I thought . . ."

"She is," that traitor Gypsy piped up. "Only she doesn't want to talk about it or even admit it."

"Oh, but you should be proud!" Helen's voice boomed. "Who else can say they're a quintuplet?" And then she laughed. "Other than your siblings. What is it, two girls, three boys?"

My face was on fire. I could feel every kid staring at me.

Gypsy piped up again. "It's three girls, two boys, isn't it, Emma?" And she repeated to Helen, "But she really doesn't like to talk about it."

I heard Corliss whisper to Dolores, "Is she really?"

Helen boomed out, "I know how you must feel—" (sure!) "—but you have to overcome a lot of things if you want to be an actor." She looked at her clipboard. "Where were we? Oh, yes. Emma, you and Stacey get up there now and pretend one of you is the mother and the other is a ten-year-old who has hidden a duck in her room."

"A *duck?*" We said it together.

"Yep."

Stacey and I looked at each other. "I'll be the mother," she said as we walked to the front of the room.

When we got there, Stacey made a rapping motion. "It's Mother, Stephanie." She pretended to open a door. "What's that funny sound coming from your room?" she asked.

"Uh . . . the TV?" I tried to make my voice sound like a ten-year-old's.

"You don't have a TV," she said. Stacey stooped and picked up an imaginary something from the floor. "Where did this feather come from?"

Without even thinking, I said, "From my duck pillow."

"But your pillow is stuffed with foam," she said.

"Oh . . . then it must have blown in through the window."

"Quack, quack," Helen said from the audience.

"Young lady, I just now heard a duck. Do you have one in this room?"

"Time!" Helen called out, to my immense relief.

Stacey and I went back to our seats.

"Your dialogue was excellent," Helen said. "It showed inventiveness and quick thinking. Now, as to characters . . ." And she went on to tell us that in a real scene we'd need to be more specific types, but that took study and planning.

When the class came to a close, Helen said we all had the makings of actors. "You're a mega-talented bunch," she said. "I wouldn't mind recommending any one of you."

"For what?" Henry asked.

"You'll find out in time," she said, gathering up her belongings. "Your assignment for this week is to watch a TV show and pick out one character in it. Then tell me how the character you chose is different from the other characters. What gestures, what expressions make him or her stand out? What do they tell you about the person's background?"

As we were leaving, Helen motioned me over. She waited until the other kids had left, except for Gypsy, who was waiting by the door.

"I'm sorry if I embarrassed you," she said. "I didn't dream that being a quint might be a sore subject."

I didn't know what to say, so I just gave a little shrug.

"What is there about it that makes you uncomfortable?"

"I just don't like being one," I mumbled.

"So you try to deny it?"

I didn't like being put on the spot this way. "My parents don't want . . . don't want us exploited."

"Emma, I'd never exploit you."

I felt my face flush. "I didn't mean . . ."

"But I'm sorry if I made you uncomfortable. I had no idea it wasn't generally known."

It could be now, I thought. "That's okay," I said.

Helen touched my shoulder. "Try to forget all that. Just concentrate on your acting. I liked what you did today, Emma. You showed you can think on your feet." She beamed at me.

"Thanks," I said. I felt a lot better as I went over to join Gypsy.

While we were unlocking our bikes, Gypsy said, "I'm going to meet Wharton at the hardware store. Want to come along?"

"Hardware store?"

"He likes to browse there."

"Oh." Weird kid. But why should I be surprised? "I'd better get home," I said. "I'm expecting a call."

"From James?"

"No, not from James." I really wasn't. "From my big sister, Natalie."

"James might be with Wharton. You ought to come along."

"I'm not . . ." I almost said *going to chase after a boy* but that would sound pretty offensive. "In the mood," I said instead.

"You still ticked about your quint cover being blown?"

"No, I'm not." I was, a little, but I wasn't about to admit it.

"Okay, then." Gypsy threw her chain and lock into the basket of her bike. "Come over tomorrow. I have to baby-sit, but not all afternoon."

"We're going to visit relatives."

"Poor you. See you Monday, then."

I did try to call Natalie, but this time even her machine didn't answer. I wandered downstairs and found Mom in the living room, kneeling on the floor and sorting through magazines.

"These things just pile up," she said. "I don't seem

to have time to read them, and yet they're too good to pitch out."

"Mom, I'm worried about Natalie. She's never home and now even her machine is off. I know this sounds creepy, but what if some pervert got into her apartment and . . ."

"Please. Don't even say it." Mom stood up. "Anyway, Natalie's in Aspen. We got a postcard."

"Skiing? In early spring?"

"I don't know. She just said she's having a great time. Do you want to go with me to the hardware store?"

I must have looked shocked.

"Emma, what's wrong with a hardware store? Are you still worrying about axe murderers, or what?"

"It's just . . . it's just . . . that Dad usually goes."

"Well, for heaven's sake." She put a hand on the back of my neck and walked me from the room. "I'm not about to send your father for a new shower curtain." And kiddingly, "He has no taste, we all know that."

"Which hardware store?"

"The new one, out at the strip mall."

"Oh. Okay." I knew Gypsy was going to the store downtown. "Do you think they'd have desk lamps? I need a new one . . . that old one of Natalie's fell apart."

On our way to the hardware store we wandered past a gigantic sports equipment shop.

"Mom, wait a minute." I stared at a display of skates in the window. "Look at all those different kinds of Rollerblades!"

"Rollerblades? I didn't know they interested you."

"It's just that they're . . ." *What James has.* "So cool looking."

"Mmmm." Mom started away and I caught up with her. But I looked back over my shoulder at the skates. Wouldn't it be fun to go skimming along in a cute shorts outfit . . . plaid, maybe . . . and with my hair streaming? And then I could almost hear Dad's voice adding, "And wiping out on a patch of gravel, with your knees bleeding and your wrist broken?"

Why did Dad have to put the damper on everything . . . even my daydreams!

As I followed Mom into the hardware store, I thought, *I'm not going to daydream about Rollerblades. I'm not the least bit interested in owning a pair. What I'm going to daydream about . . . if I do it at all . . . is becoming really good at acting. If I were good at that, it would set me apart from my brothers and sisters. People wouldn't think of me as a quint, but as a superb performer.*

When we walked out of the store a while later, loaded down with the shower curtain, lamp, and a few other things we couldn't live without, we passed by the window with the Rollerblades again. I gave them a glance and again had the vision of my very own self rolling along in wild abandon. I could do it. I could do that right away. Becoming famous for acting, however, might take a long, long time.

CHAPTER 8

*O*n Monday at noon, I stopped by my locker on the way to the cafeteria to change shoes. I'd worn a new pair of patents but decided to switch to some old loafers for the afternoon. As I straightened up I saw Jenny and Shari standing there. What did they want, I wondered. I hardly knew them.

"Is it true?" Shari asked.

"True? What?"

"That you're a quint?"

I caught my breath, unable to answer.

"See, Emma's blushing. It's true," Jenny said. "I told you."

"Well, how come no one knew about it before?" Shari gave me a suspicious look, as though I were someone in a TV show, guilty of withholding vital information.

"H-how do you know?" I managed to stammer. "Who told you?"

"It's all over school," Jenny said.

"What is?" Gypsy had suddenly appeared.

The girls looked a bit cowed. Gypsy was wearing her don't-mess-with-me look. Then Jenny ventured, "Everyone's talking about her"—she glanced at me—"being a quint. And we thought . . ."

"You thought, huh?" Gypsy blew out her breath. "It must get noisy up there, one little thought rattling around in that void."

Shari plucked at Jenny's sleeve. "Let's go. We don't have to stand here and listen to this. Especially from . . ." She gave Gypsy a look of disgust. *From these inferior beings*, they might as well have said. They turned and left, talking to each other, and pausing once to look back . . . probably to see if we were both squished.

I slammed my locker shut. Damn. For a couple of years hardly anyone had been aware that Beth and I . . . the only ones in this school . . . were even related. I wondered if the kids had gotten to her, too.

"We almost made it to graduation," I said to Gypsy. "I wonder who blew our cover." And then it struck us simultaneously. *"Dolores!"* From acting class!

"She must have raced home and set up a phone marathon," I said. "I'm skipping lunch."

"Don't be crazy," Gypsy said. "You can't pull a fade for the rest of the term."

"Yeah, you're right." I dragged down the hall. "I'd like to throttle that Dolores, though. She always seemed so sweet and simpleminded, and now she turns out to be a viper."

"A viper, maybe, but I have to say she's a standout in acting class."

I stopped. "I can't believe this. You're defending her!"

"I'm not. I'm just saying she's a good actor, possibly with few scruples. A fact that may take her far in the theater."

As we reached the cafeteria, Gypsy stopped me. "What do you plan to do . . . deny?"

"Yes, sure. Deny that I was born."

"Well . . . what's going to be your attitude?"

"I'm going to rise above it."

"There you go!"

Actually, it wasn't too bad. There were a few looks and whispers, but most of the kids had left or were leaving by the time we got to the cafeteria. We got the remains of lunch, which I hardly touched, but which Gypsy gobbled up, as always.

* * *

When I got home Beth and Alice were waiting for me in the kitchen. "So how come you told everybody?" Beth didn't even have to tell me what.

"I didn't tell anybody." I opened the refrigerator. I was starving.

"Then how come it's all over school?"

There was nothing in the refrigerator. I opened the freezer and took out a package of frozen waffles. "Dolores found out accidentally at acting class."

"Dolores Travers? Little Miss Is-There-Life-Hidden-Within?"

"The same." I dropped two waffles into the toaster. "What did you say to the kids?"

61

"I told them to mind their own business."

"What a great comeback," I said.

"The point is, as I see it," Alice said in her most sisterly manner, "the quint thing is now out in the open."

I didn't answer. I knew Alice would go on anyway.

"So we might as well roll with it."

"Yeah? Meaning what?" I got the butter and syrup ready.

"Meaning that since people know, we might as well go public."

Beth frowned. "Alice, you make it sound like some scandal."

"All I'm saying is, what's the harm now in letting the media cover our graduation? It would show people that, yes, we're quints and we're proud of it."

"You go on and be proud," I said, "but you'd better make it quadruplets because I won't go along."

"You can't resign from being a quint," Alice said. "That's impossible."

"You're impossible," I said. "And I'm sick of the subject!" I stormed from the room, forgetting all about the waffles.

"Oh, come on back," Alice called. "Don't be such a drag!"

And then I heard Beth say, "Want one of these waffles, Alice?"

* * *

When we all gathered for dinner, I could tell that the girls had told Drew and Craig. The boys gave me these looks that said, *Is she going to explode?* When I acted natural, they went back to behaving the way they usually do at the table . . . like a pair of bear cubs on a food rampage.

For Dad, things had gone right at work for a change, so he was in a good mood. He even kidded Alice and Beth a little about their super-blond hair. "I knew you two were going to turn into flutter-brains from the time you first learned to talk," he said. That's Dad's way of making friendly conversation. My sisters weren't the least bit offended.

"What about Emma?" Craig asked.

"Emma?" Dad looked at me as though I'd just joined the family. "Emma's more like Natalie." Then he turned to Mom. "Speaking of Natalie, have you heard any more from her? I wonder what she was doing in Aspen. Doesn't she have a job?"

"She probably had sick days coming, so she took off for a long weekend," Mom said. "Some people do take time off, you know."

"Yeah, Dad, not like you," Craig said. "You act like the whole airport would close down if you weren't there for a few days."

"I'm satisfied with my three weeks," he said. "You guys start thinking of where we might go this summer."

"Camping," Craig said.

"Other than that."

"What do you have against nature?" Drew demanded. "Don't you think it would be great to sleep out under the stars?"

"Only if there's a roof over my head."

"Your father's idea of roughing it is to stay at a Holiday Inn, you know that," Mom said, as she got up to pour coffee.

The girls then suggested going to Hawaii and the boys to Australia.

"How about you, Emma?" Mom asked. "Where would you like to go?"

Somewhere alone. "It doesn't matter," I said.

Dad picked up on my mood. "What's wrong with you, Emmykins?"

"Nothing. I just don't care."

There was a moment of silence. I thought of blurting out what had happened at school, but I didn't. Why spoil a friendly atmosphere?

As though he had pulled it out of the air, Dad said, "Of course, taking all you guys together would be a problem."

"Why?" Alice asked innocently.

Dad just looked at her. "You know why."

"Don't you think it's about time to let people know about us?" Alice answered.

"No, I don't."

"What if . . ." Alice thought better of it. "Oh, never mind."

For just a second, our eyes met. But that second told me somehow that Alice wasn't giving up. I had to admire her spirit, if not her good sense. Didn't she know there was no way she'd win this one?

* * *

In my room, I dialed Natalie's number for about the sixth time since she'd left a message for me. It was almost a shock when she answered.

"You're back!" I said.

"Sad to say, I am."

"Did you have a good time in Aspen?"

"The greatest."

"Did you ski?"

"No snow."

"Oh. Then what did you do?"

"Emma, can you keep a secret?"

For a moment I wavered. But I wasn't the one who'd told about our being quints. "Sure. What kind of secret?"

"Emma, guess who I met at Aspen?"

"Kevin Costner."

"No, you nit. Someone you've met."

I couldn't think of anyone I'd met who was all that great.

"Noel," she finally told me.

"Noel?" Natalie's old boyfriend. "So? You've been seeing him off and on for years. What was so special about this time?"

"Emma . . . promise me you won't tell?"

"Sure. I promise."

"Well . . ." I could almost hear my half-sister take a deep breath. "We're engaged."

"Engaged!" I yelped.

"Ssshhhh. Yes. We decided. We're going to get married this summer."

"Wow! Natalie!"

"And there's something I want to ask you. Would you like to be my maid of honor?"

I gasped.

"Emma? Are you there?"

"Me? You want *me?*"

"Well, why not? We've always been so close."

"I just don't know what to say!"

"Well, don't say anything . . . not to the others. I want to come there and tell Dad and Jean in person."

"When?"

"I'm not sure. I just couldn't wait to tell you. But be sure to be surprised when I do break the news."

"Does anyone else know? Besides Noel, of course."

"I told my mom. She's pleased."

"I'm so excited!"

"Well, cool down. And Emma, don't even tell your best friend. Dad would have a fit if he heard about the engagement from someone else."

I thought of telling Natalie about the quint secret spilling out at school. Then I decided not to. What had happened in my life couldn't compare with this news of hers.

I went to sleep that night thinking of the wedding. Would Natalie go the whole route, white gown, veil, big ceremony? It didn't seem her style. Her mother might want her to, though. After all, Natalie was her only daughter . . . her only child.

I dreamed that the wedding took place in our front yard. There were streamers all across the front, like they have at used car lots. And Natalie came roaring down the driveway wearing a long white wedding gown . . . and Rollerblades.

Sometimes dreams are about as substantial as smoke. They drift away once you're awake. But this dream stayed with me the next day. I could still see Natalie in her wedding gown. That part of the dream would come true. And about the Rollerblades . . . maybe that would come true as well. It would, I decided. I'd make sure it did.

CHAPTER 9

I thought about Natalie's wedding so much the next few days, and the part I was going to play in it, that even Gypsy noticed.

"What is it with you, anyway?" she asked. "You act like Cinderella on overtime. Have you been talking to James, or what?"

"James?"

"Yes, James. The guy who likes you."

"Likes me?" And then it registered. "He *likes* me? How do you know?"

"Because he told Wharton, and Wharton . . . you know the drill."

I nudged Gypsy in warning. We were in the gym locker rooms, suiting up for tennis instruction . . . it was that time of year. Kids were going back and forth with antennas fully extended, the way they do if there's even a hint of boy-talk in the air.

"Tell me later," I said in a lowered voice. Danielle Motley had turned away suddenly when I looked up. I wondered how much she'd heard.

"I hear the entire team of boys wants to score love points with you," Gypsy said in a carrying voice.

"*Gypsy!*"

"I'm talking tennis!" Gypsy exclaimed. "What did you think, Danielle?"

"Stop it, Gypsy."

"I'm just having fun." Danielle was walking rapidly away. "Giving them something to talk about."

Sometimes it seemed to me that my best friend and I were playing tug-of-war, with her pulling for attention at any price and me trying to keep in the shadows.

My court performance that day was not great. I didn't seem able to anticipate the returns. I felt sorry for my partner.

"Where's your concentration, Wentworth?" the coach called out after I missed another easy shot. "You've got to keep focused."

"Sorry," I said to my partner, a girl named Sally, as we walked back to the gym.

"Hey, everyone has off days," she said, bouncing a tennis ball up and down on her racquet as we went along. "But you have great coordination. You should go out for gymnastics in high school."

Inside, there was a wild scramble for the showers. As I stood with the water streaming over me I thought about what Sally had said. Did I want to compete . . . put myself in the limelight that way? Then I had to smile. What about acting? That was really calling attention to myself.

It just seemed that so much was going around in my head. Drama class, Natalie's wedding, James. But

James was on hold. I might not ever see him or talk to him again, in spite of how Gypsy went on about him.

* * *

He called me that night.

I was in Beth and Alice's room at the time. We were doing our weekly clothes-trading-around thing. It was even more challenging tonight because there were a few new things Mom had let us pick up at the mall.

Alice was trying on the blue top that I hoped she wouldn't like, because I did, when the phone rang. "It's probably Randy," she said just before picking it up. "Hi, weasel." Then she looked startled. "Oh . . . sorry. Just a sec." She held the phone toward me and mouthed, "It's a guy."

"A guy?" Beth squealed.

I put my hand over the mouthpiece. "Shut up, you two."

They looked at each other, flopped their hands in the air, and said, "Wooo—ooo."

"Yeah, it's Emma," I said into the phone.

"Who was that who answered?" James asked.

"Just one of my stupid sisters."

"You got a lot?"

"Two. Too many." And then, before he could get into the age question, I asked, "Do you have any sisters?"

The looks on Alice and Beth's faces said *boring!* They made the speed-it-up motion.

I walked the long cord through the bathroom and into my own room, and closed and locked the door.

"No sisters, one younger brother," James was saying.

"That's nice." I didn't know how to go on from there.

"I hear you're taking acting lessons," he said. "That's cool. What do you want to be, in the movies?"

"I think that would be a stretch," I said.

"How come?"

"Well . . . it takes a lot of talent . . . and . . ."

"You've got the looks."

My legs felt funny. I sat down on the floor. "I do?"

"You should know that you do. Haven't you ever looked in a mirror?"

For the first time I was sorry our phone didn't have an extension. I wouldn't have minded having my sisters hear this. Without thinking, I said, "You should see my sisters."

"Why?"

"Because . . . well, they're the ones with the looks."

"Come one, don't give me that."

I wasn't going to argue. "Are you still Rollerblading?"

"Every chance I get. You should try it." Pause. "Want to?"

"I don't have the skates."

"I could borrow my brother's. He's about your size. Just to try, see if you like it."

I felt shivery. Nicely shivery. "When?"

"Maybe after you finish class Saturday? I could meet you there. I know where it is. Wharton told me."

"Okay." Just like that. *Okay.* What was I thinking of!

"All right, then. See you Saturday."

I sat on the floor for a few minutes filled with a feeling of wonder. A boy . . . a cute boy . . . thought I was movie-star pretty. Wow. Me, Emma. The quiet one. The non-blond one.

This was too good to keep quiet. I got up and took the phone back into the girls' room.

"Well?" they said together. "Give!"

"It's just a kid I know." *Who thinks I'm cool.* "We have a date Saturday." I knew this was probably not smart, but I had to gloat just a little.

"A date? A real date? Dad'll have a fit! That's great, Emma!"

"It's just to go Rollerblading, so don't make a lot of it."

"But Emma, it's your first time!" Alice tossed the blue top to me. "Want a few pointers?"

"I'll manage." I knew, Beth knew, and Drew and Craig knew that Alice had had several dates, but also in the afternoons and without the folks knowing. "You still sneaking out to see what's-his-name?"

"Tony. And no, I'm not seeing him. We broke up. He's a jerk." Alice held up an amber-striped top. "I'll take this one for tomorrow. Or no, maybe that red over there."

"I'm wearing it," Beth said. "So you can wear it next. Then next week Emma, if you want to." Since Beth and I were in the same school, we always let a little time go by before wearing what the other had worn. It had become routine.

I tried on the blue and checked it out in the mirror

with Beth standing by. And then I realized something that must have been going on for some time. I was growing! I don't mean that I'd ever been all that much shorter, but still I'd always been the runt of the litter.

"Beth, look," I said. I pulled her next to me. "I'm almost as tall as you are."

Beth looked a bit puzzled. "But when did this happen? Look, Alice. Look at Emma."

Alice did, and gave a motherly sigh. "Our little girl is growing up."

They went back to the clothes. From the corner of my eye I noticed Alice making a little signal to Beth. I whirled around.

"What is it?" I asked. "What's going on?"

"Uh, Emma . . ." Alice gave me a sweet little smile that made me suspicious. "Beth and I decided . . ." She gave Beth a look. "Since you and the boys seem to get along . . ."

"*Boys*? There's only one."

"I mean our brothers." She took a deep breath. "Maybe you could convince them to go along with the TV thing."

"Are you still on that? Give it up!"

Alice wasn't about to. "Look, Emma. The kids at school know all about our being quints, and it's because of your acting class. So in a way, you're responsible."

"I am not! The teacher blurted it out!"

"Whatever. Anyway, that's how the word got around. So you might as well profit from it."

"Profit! You're a loon, Alice."

Beth moved a little closer. "It could help you, being on TV, in your career as an actor. I mean, any kind of exposure . . ."

"Who's exposing what?" Drew asked as he and Craig, followed by Sylvester, came into the room. "Are we talking cameras here?"

"TV cameras," Alice said.

"Not that again." Craig gave her a look of disgust.

"Why not?" Beth asked. Obviously, she'd been brainwashed by her sister.

"Because," Craig answered.

"Oh, very clever." Alice rolled her eyes. *"Because.* I must remember that intelligent word."

"If we all banded together," Beth said, scratching Sylvester around his collar, "and told the folks that's what we want, to be on TV, they might give in."

Craig turned to me. "Is it what you want?"

"No."

Alice glared at me. "I'll say it again. You're responsible for blowing the quint cover, whether you want to admit it or not."

"You *told?*" Drew asked.

Furious, I got up to leave.

As I reached the door, Alice yelled, "You needn't think you're so above it all, just because you have some jerk boyfriend!"

I slammed the door behind me. At that moment I really despised my sister.

After about ten minutes there was a knock on my door and Drew looked in.

"Emma, come on back, will you?"

"Why should I?"

"We're trying to plan something for vacation."

"Go ahead. You don't need me."

"We've got to stick together."

"Ha!"

"Come on, Emma." Drew smiled in the same way Mom does. It's a smile I can't resist. I got up and went back to the girls' room.

As we walked in, the others acted as though nothing had happened. Craig was saying, "How do you feel about river rafting? Shooting the rapids?"

"Give me a break," Alice said.

"You'd never get me on one of those things," Beth said.

"Emma?"

"It sounds like fun, but Dad wouldn't go. You know how he is about nature. He thinks it's unnatural."

"Maybe we'll split up again," Beth said. "Mom might want to go somewhere civilized like San Francisco. Or Hawaii. The girls could go with her." Suddenly she snapped her fingers. "I know! We could get Natalie to go with us! You know how well she and Mom have always gotten along, and of course she adores us!"

Now Craig made the gagging sound, with gestures.

"I don't think—" I stopped. "I mean, Natalie probably has already planned her . . . uh, vacation." I almost said *honeymoon*.

"No harm in asking," Beth said.

"Remember when Natalie was here, when we were about five?" Craig said, dragging a pillow off Beth's bed and doubling it under his head as he sprawled on the floor. "When she and Mom and Dad took us to the zoo, and one of us got lost?"

"I think it was you, Craig," Alice said. "Didn't they find you in a cage with the rest of the apes?"

"Thanks. Speaking of getting lost, remember the time Great-aunt Toots and Uncle Horace took a couple of us in their RV to Colorado and we *all* got lost and ended up in Texas? That turned out to be a great trip."

"Aunt Toots must be lonely now that Uncle Horace is dead," Beth said.

Craig gave a laugh. "How could she get lonely with all those birds?"

"But still," Alice persisted. "It's so sad when someone close to you . . . I mean . . . I'd just die if Mom or Dad or any of you . . ."

She looked up at me then, and her look seemed to say *I'm sorry*. I couldn't stay angry at Alice. She's a pain at times, but she's my sister. My quint sister. We'd been together even before we were born.

I think there in that room, at that moment, we all felt the bond of our birth. Our shared memories were probably stronger than those of most brothers and sisters, because we were all the same age when the events happened.

After a while the boys drifted off and I gathered up my stack of clothes and went to my room. For a while I diddled around, printing James's name in various ways but still not linking it with mine, and finally got down to homework.

It wasn't until later, when I lay in bed, that my thoughts went back to summer vacation and then to

Natalie. *Natalie's getting married!* It was such a strange yet wonderful thought. And I was to have a featured role in the ceremony . . . me, Emma, the maid of honor!

But then, without wanting to, I saw the other quints' faces . . . how they'd look, from a distance, watching, not a part of it. I felt a pull toward them, and an opposite pull toward Natalie.

But this wasn't fair. I didn't need to feel any doubts, any dragging back and forth. It was Natalie's wedding and she could run it the way she wanted. So there! I switched the bedside light back on and picked up the book I'd been reading. Losing a little sleep this way was at least better than lying awake, thinking.

But I couldn't concentrate. The thought of my Saturday date with James kept coming back into my mind. When I began seeing his face on the margin of the book, I gave up even trying to read.

CHAPTER 10

I met James after class on Saturday. True to his word, he had an extra pair of Rollerblades with him and knee guards, too. I rode my bike and he skated along to a stretch of sidewalk in front of some vacant lots.

"I was afraid you'd drag along your friend . . . what's her name?" James asked.

"Gypsy. She had to go home and sister-sit." She'd made me promise to remember every single word we said. I couldn't tell if she was impressed with my date, or envious. So far, she hadn't actually gone out with Wharton.

James was so patient I couldn't believe it. When I was laced into the Rollerblades, which were only a tad too big, he got out of his and walked along in his socks to support my first try.

I was so nervous and shaky, it was a good thing James had his feet on solid sidewalk. After going back and forth a few times, though, I seemed to pick up energy and confidence. I stopped shaking.

"You're doing really well," James said. "You sure this is your first time?"

"On these. I know how to ice skate, though."

"That puts you ahead of the game. Think you can go it alone, now, if I put mine back on?"

"I think so."

It was great. After a while I wanted to skate farther, but I had to keep an eye on my bike. Also there was always a chance I'd run into someone I knew . . . an adult, I mean, who might innocently say something to my parents.

"You have a birthday coming up?" James suddenly asked.

"No, it's later on in the year."

"Too bad. I was thinking you might hit up your folks for a pair of blades."

I sat down on the curb and took off the knee guards and skates. When I stood up my legs felt strange, as though they realized they'd plunged down a couple of inches. "Thanks," I said, handing back the Roller-blades. "It was really fun."

"You have to go home now?"

"It isn't that I have to go home," I said. "But I thought I'd stop by to see my Great-aunt Toots."

"Toots? That's her name?"

I laughed. "It's Thelma, but no one has ever called her that. Toots is a case. She's always been on the wacky side, but now she's really gone out of control. She has birds."

"Birds? What kind of birds?"

"You name 'em, she's got 'em." I unlocked my bike and tossed the chain in the basket. "She started out with a few, but now they've taken over the whole house. It's squawk city."

"Where does she live?"

"Just on the outskirts. Past the Kmart a few blocks." I suddenly didn't want to leave James. "Would you like to come along?" And then I realized. "But you couldn't skate all the way, the roads aren't all that good, and there aren't sidewalks. I wish you could come, though."

"How about if I skated as far as possible, and then pedaled your bike, with you on the crossbar?"

"Okay." More than ever I was glad I'd chosen a boy's model when we all got bikes.

When we reached the end of the sidewalk, James took off his skates and put them into the basket along with the pair I'd worn. I began to feel a little worried. Here I was, about to ride sidesaddle on a bike pedaled by a kid I hardly knew.

James seemed expert, though. After a bit I stopped gripping the center of the handlebar so hard. Then I released one hand because I had to pull my long hair to the side and hold it to keep it from flying in his face. I imagined I could feel his breath on the back of my exposed neck. It was unlike any feeling I'd ever had before. Warm. Close.

"There's her house," I said finally, pointing with the elbow of the hand holding my hair. It was a good thing Toots's house was isolated, considering the racket her birds made.

When we got to the yard, which was pretty much overgrown with weeds, I got off the bike and James walked it to the porch.

"Oh, hey, I forgot. You're in your socks," I said.

"Does that embarrass you? I could wait outside."

"I was thinking of the bird-you-know-what. Be careful where you step."

"The birds are loose?"

"Some are. Watch your head, too."

James laughed. "Are you putting me on?"

"Just wait." I knocked. And waited. And knocked again.

"Keep your shirt on!" a voice screeched. "I'm a-comin'."

Great-aunt Toots was never dressed in anything you'd expect to see on a woman of seventy-something (Dad said the secret of the exact number of years was hidden in Fort Knox). As far as this aunt and clothes were concerned, every day was Halloween.

Today the top half of her didn't seem to go with the bottom half. Her gray hair, dangling in a big braid at the back, was fastened with a huge red satin bow that looked as though it had come off a Christmas wreath. And it may well have. Her blouse was white with red polka dots and a ruffly neckline. With it she was wearing camouflage army pants and combat boots she must have found at an old Army-Navy store.

"Why, Emma!" she said, throwing her arms around me. "Li'l darlin', I'm so thrilled to see you!"

"Me, too," I said. "Aunt Toots, this is . . ."

"Why, boy, I'd know you anywhere!" she said,

throwing her arms around James while he stood there off-balance, smiling shakily. "But give me some help here. Are you Craig or—let's see—Drew?"

"It's not a brother," I said. "It's James . . . a friend of mine."

"Oh, I see. Are you two sweethearts?" She gave me a playful nudge.

"A friend," I repeated, wishing I could dematerialize.

"Well, you can count on your old Aunt Toots not to broadcast it around. Why don't you come on in?" She held the screen door open wide and I was surprised no birds came swooping out.

When we got inside the living room, which had not one stick of furniture in it other than a couple of floor lamps, I saw the birds were all in cages. "Come on in, see my pretties," Aunt Toots said.

I gave James a look but his gaze was fastened on an especially large cage. "Wow!" he said. "What kind of birds are those?"

"They're turacos," Toots said. "Those two there are white-crested and that other one is an Angola red-crested. Aren't they handsome?"

"Fantastic. Where do they come from?"

"Africa. Now these birds next to the window are cockatiels. The albino is very rare. I call him Whitey, and the pearly one here is—guess what? Pearly."

"Do you give them all names?" James asked, moving to the next cage.

"Just the ones with outstanding personalities," Toots said.

She went on, saying this one was a Java hill mynah,

that one a white-bearded honeyeater. She explained that one really noisy, ugly bird with a huge beak was a great barbet, all the way from the Himalayan region. I was beginning to feel sorry for James. He looked interested, but then you can never tell with polite types.

I opened a door out to the hall, and Toots called out, "Be careful, I'm exercisin' some of them!"

I ducked my head as a squadron of squawking birds flew out of formation overhead. They barely landed on a rod at one end of the hall before they whirled around, fluttered their wings, and came zooming back. One almost flew into James's face as he walked into the hall.

"Be careful," Toots called out. "These birds are delicate."

"Like buzzards," I said, stepping out of the path of a low-flyer. "Why are they so revved up?"

"Because they're caged a lot of the time. This is their way of working off steam."

"One of my aunts has a parakeet, but she always keeps it in the cage," James said.

"Well, no aspersions on your aunt," Toots said. "She's probably a nice woman otherwise. But it's downright cruel to cage up a little bird night and day. You might hint that to her, next time you're at her house."

"She lives in Louisiana."

"Oh. Well, then, why don't you send her a postcard?"

"Want to see the rest of them?" I asked James, to change the subject.

"There're *more*?"

Toots laughed. "Laddie, you haven't seen but the start of my birds. Here, let me light this hall light so you can see where you're walking. Especially since you've got no shoes on."

It was a good thing she warned him. The floor was covered with newspapers and it was hard to see the white and black splotches against the newsprint. James walked very carefully.

The spare bedroom had no bed, but lots of cages. Toots closed the door behind us because a few birds were flying around.

"Sweetie and Snookums are restless girls," Toots said, holding out an arm. One of the birds—I didn't know it by name—landed and began pecking at her Mickey Mouse watch.

"Now, none of that, Sweetie," Toots said, holding out a finger of her other hand. The bird hopped on it and, to my great disgust, kissed Toots on command. Well, touched her beak to her lips. "See why I call her Sweetie?" Toots said. "Now, go back in your cage, that's a good girl."

The other bedroom did have a four-poster and a chest of drawers and a nightstand. There were only three cages in there.

We walked out to the kitchen. It was full of parrots. James jumped as a big yellow and red and blue number flew past his left ear and landed on top of the refrigerator. From there, the bird's beady eyes seemed to be scoping out where he should land next. James and I backed away.

"Johnny, you rascal," Toots said. "Behave yourself. These kiddos don't understand your playful ways."

Under my breath I said, "Like plucking out an eyeball here and there."

Toots opened a cupboard, got out a box of bird cookies, and scattered a few on the counter. With great squawkings and battings of colored wings, parrots zapped in from all directions, scrambling and fighting for the goodies. Toots grabbed one particularly vicious character and put him in a cage. Then, softhearted, she shoved a cookie through the bars.

I glanced at James, who had cupped his hands around his eyes to shield them.

Aunt Toots yanked off a paper towel and cleaned up a spot on the counter. "Don't think I let them make a mess of things all the time," she said. "I try to keep the place up."

"You do a good job, Aunt Toots," I said, "considering . . . uh . . . that you have so many birds."

"I get the feeling that some people stay away just because they think it's not natural . . . you know, keeping birds this way."

"Really?"

"Yes, they do. Your father for instance, Emma. He came out and said I ought to get rid of them. That they carry disease. I don't know what's wrong with him, talking that way."

"I guess he just doesn't know them the way you do."

"Say, would you kids like some cookies and milk?" She opened the same cupboard door and scooted boxes around. "Seems like I had some cookies in here somewhere."

"No thanks, we've . . ." James stammered.

"We've got to go," I finished for him. "I just wanted to stop by and see how you are."

"Well, you're a sweetheart for doin' it, and Craig . . ."

"James . . ."

"James . . . that's what I said . . . you come back real soon."

We walked carefully back down the hall to the front door. Aunt Toots kissed me on the cheek and told me to tell everyone hello, and to James she said, "Now, don't forget to send your aunt a postcard about letting that bird out of the cage."

"Right away," James promised. He checked the soles of his socks but he hadn't stepped in anything. I didn't know how he'd avoided it.

Outside, I said, "Well, that's my Great-aunt Toots."

"She's, uh . . . an unusual lady," James said.

"To put it mildly. I really like her, though."

"So do I," James said. "She's real."

* * *

At home I suddenly felt very uneasy. I should have told Toots not to mention James if she talked to my folks. But that would have sounded as though I was sneaking around . . . which I was, in a way. Besides, she'd said she wouldn't broadcast it. But she might forget and say something and then get flustered and make it worse.

I decided I'd better tell Mom, just to be on the safe

side. She happened to be in my room when I got there, putting some clean clothes into my dresser drawer.

When I told her about going to visit Toots, she said, "You rode out there on your bike, all alone?"

"It's not all that far," I said. I took a breath. "Besides, a boy went with me. It was right after acting class. Gypsy had to go home or she would've come along."

"How is your aunt?"

I exhaled. Mom must not have picked up on what I'd said. "She's fine. More birds than ever."

Mom gave a little sigh. "I wonder if that's good for her."

"She seems okay." And then, just when I relaxed, Mom turned and asked, "Was it a boy from your acting class?"

"Wh . . . who?"

"You said a boy went with you."

"Oh. No. That was James."

"James who?"

For a moment I panicked. Then I remembered his last name. "James Davies."

"Where did you meet him?"

"Mom . . . what is this? Am I on the witness stand or something?"

"Emma, where did you meet this boy?"

I slumped onto my bed. "If I tell you, you'll tell Dad, and you know what a ruckus he always makes."

Mom sat down beside me. "Is it someone you're ashamed of?"

"No! He's nice, Mom, really nice. You'd like him. I just met him in a funny way. He was Rollerblading where Gypsy and I were logging in a move and we all started talking and . . ."

"And?"

"And he called me a couple of times and said he'd teach me to Rollerblade."

"And did he?" I nodded. "Where?"

"Downtown, on the sidewalk in front of where the stores burned last year . . ."

"Harvard Street?"

"Yeah. And Mom, I was really good. I caught on fast. It's so much fun. Do you think I could get a pair?"

"Let's hear the rest of the story. So you were Rollerblading and then you went to Toots's house?"

"That's right." There was no need to worry Mom by telling her how the two of us had gone on one bike. That could get me grounded. "And she thought at first that James was Craig . . . he looks a little bit like him."

"Well, Emma, I wish you'd told me about this before. About your . . . friend, I mean. I'd like to think you trust me. Just as I trust you."

That bit a little. "Dad wouldn't understand, though."

"Your father doesn't like to think you're all growing up and will leave someday."

"I should think he'd be glad for the peace and quiet."

"He might even say so, but I know better. He really felt bad when Natalie moved back with her mother."

"Do you think he loved her more than he loves us?"

"Oh, Emma." Mom pulled my head against her shoulder. "Of course not. But she was his eldest, remember. They'd been together for thirteen years. And you five were babies, just beginning to talk. He loves every one of you, but in a different way."

"So are you going to tell him about James?"

Mom got up. "No, honey, you'd better tell him yourself. Or better yet, bring the boy over to the house. If he's as nice as you say, I can't think your father would have a howling fit. But you understand . . . no dates. You're too young for that." She turned at the door. I got up and left the room with her.

I wouldn't have minded having James over at the house. But there was one big problem. He didn't know I was a quint. I didn't want him to know. Sometimes when people found out about us they started treating us like a five-part person instead of as individuals. I couldn't believe James would be that way, but I didn't want to take a chance. Not so soon. I wanted to impress myself upon his mind as Emma . . . just Emma . . . a very special friend.

CHAPTER 11

I should have stayed upstairs with Mom, but instead I went down to the living room. Just as I entered, Dad rattled the newspaper and said, "Well, this is hard to believe."

"What, Dad?" Beth asked, looking up from the comics.

"It says here that students today are so ignorant about geography they can't even locate Germany on a map. In fact, they can't locate the oceans. They think Philadelphia is a state."

Craig walked into the room. "Can you locate the Indian Ocean?" Dad shot out at him.

"I don't know. Is it lost?"

"See?" Dad slapped his leg. "Smart replies, but no smart answers." He turned toward Beth and me. "How about you two? Do you have the faintest idea where the Indian Ocean is located? And please don't tell me Indiana."

Beth tried logic. "It's by India. Isn't it?"

"Too obvious. All right, where's New Zealand? Craig, surely you know where that is."

"Far," Craig said.

"Could you be a bit more specific?" Dad said. I wished I could ease out of the room. Every once in a while Dad goes on a crusade, and it looked as if he was headed for one now. He had that fixed, crazed gaze.

"You thinking of going there, or what?" Craig asked, hoping, as we could all tell, to change the subject.

Dad gave a snort. "Well, if I did, I wouldn't want you as my guide. It's pretty obvious we'd never get there."

"It's no big deal," Craig said. "I'd just buy a plane ticket and let the airline worry about getting me there."

"Dad, I know where Philadelphia is," Beth said.

Dad just looked at her. Then after a moment he said, "Well, the schools may have fallen down on the job, but I'm going to see to it that you lunkheads can locate the countries of the world."

Craig and Beth and I exchanged *Oh, no* glances.

"It's just that we have so much else to learn at school," Craig said. "The whole world has expanded and gotten smaller."

"What?" Dad and I said.

"I mean," Craig rested a foot on the arm of a chair, "there's more stuff being discovered all the time in science, and communication is more advanced so it brings the world together more."

"You may be right, though that's a convoluted way

of putting it," Dad said. But then, just as Craig was looking smug, Dad went on to say, "That's no excuse though, for . . ."

"Ignorance!" the three of us said, knowing the routine.

"Right. So I'm bringing home a globe tomorrow and you kids are going to study it and be able to locate the continents, oceans, countries, states, provinces, if it takes all summer."

"Great," Craig muttered.

Alice, who had just picked up on the word *summer* as she came into the room, asked, "Oh, are we making vacation plans?"

Dad shook the paper. "I may drop you guys off in the next suburb and see if you can find your way home. Without a guide!" He went back to reading.

The four of us eased out of the room.

"What's with him?" Alice asked.

"He's on one of his holy missions," Craig said. "We have to learn geography."

"Oh, yuk." Alice turned back toward the stairs. "Emma, you have a phone call. Your wild pash."

"James?"

"There's more than one? Wooo—oo."

I raced ahead of the others. The phone was in the girls' room as usual. I dragged it into mine.

James wanted to know if I'd go skating again on Saturday. I told him I'd have to see. Privately, I was thinking I'd want my own skates if this was going to go on. But how to manage that? I didn't know. He said he'd stop by my acting class.

"Okay. Wait out front," I said. Even if Helen allowed visitors, there was no way I wanted this boy to see me doing acting exercises . . . some of them quite weird unless you were actually involved.

Hanging up, I wondered, how could I get skates? No birthday in sight. Graduation! Yes! I'd ask the folks for an early present.

Safety in numbers. That phrase came to me. The issue here wasn't safety, but persuasion. I'd have a better chance if several of us approached Mom and Dad at the same time. I asked the sibs.

Alice and Beth said they didn't know what they wanted. Craig shrugged and said he wanted to wait until Dad was in a better mood and then hit him for something major. My pal Drew said he actually would like Rollerblades himself. He was willing to make the approach with me . . . but only when the time seemed right.

I decided to make a test approach to Mom, while she was putting some papers in her briefcase. "I know it's early for a graduation gift," I ended, "but I'd get so much good out of the blades now . . . when it's spring and everything."

"Oh, honey." Mom lifted a wisp of hair that was stuck to my cheek. "Are you sure you want sports equipment? I was thinking more along the lines of jewelry . . . something you could enjoy for a long, long time."

I was tempted. Then I thought of the fun I could have skating. "I can always get a bracelet or ring," I told her, "but I'd rather have skates when I'm young . . . when my bones aren't brittle." I was thinking of one of Dad's aunts, and the way she was always breaking something.

"Well, put that way . . ." Mom said, smiling.

"I can? We can? Drew and I?"

"Hold it. I'll have to talk to your father. Or why don't you? Why always put me in the middle?"

"Because you're so experienced."

"Oh, please. No . . ." Mom went back to her papers. "You ask him. If he throws you out of the room, I'll come pick you up."

I clicked my tongue and paused, but I could see this was one of those times my mother was *taking a stand*. I hated those times.

Drew and I did go to Dad. It was just wonderful. We got a lecture about how we were spoiled rotten, how we thought we should have anything that came along, how money doesn't grow on trees (really! he actually said it), and most of all how we were such dunderheads he wasn't even sure we'd graduate.

When we left the room I told Drew, "Bad timing. He's still mad about New Zealand."

I didn't call James that week and he didn't call me again. Maybe he was already tired of me.

Having convinced myself that James and I were history, it was surprising to see him waiting outside the laundromat on Saturday.

"How was class?" he asked Gypsy and me.

"A gas," Gypsy said. "We did some inanimate objects. My best was being bubble gum."

"How did you do that?"

"You don't want to know," I told James. And then to Gypsy, "Why do we have to do auditions next week? Who needs them?"

"We will. Auditions are the meat and bones of getting anywhere in the acting world." Gypsy unlocked her bike. "So you'd better get a grip and learn to do it."

Helen, our drama coach, came out with the usual plastic basket full of laundry. "You're lookin' good, girls," she said. "Now work hard on your audition monologues this week. I want to see star talent blazing away next Saturday."

"In your dreams," I muttered as I turned toward my own bike. And then, after Helen was out of earshot, "I may just skip next week."

"Why would you do that?" Gypsy looked threatening. "You're not going to wimp out just because . . ."

"Just because everyone else is better."

Gypsy leaned her bike against the post. "Now, you don't know that."

"I know that Corliss and Dolores are a lot better than I am. Than I'll ever be."

"I'll bet you're great," James said.

I went on, "And if those two can out-act me, then I'm hopeless. I might as well give up."

"Talk to her, James," Gypsy said.

James looked confused.

"Tell her how good she is."

"But . . ."

"How's he supposed to know?" I glared at Gypsy and then wheeled my bike into the street. "I can't go skating," I said to James. "No skates."

"That's okay. We can just hang out somewhere. Want to go to the mall?"

"Great!" Gypsy said. "I've got to go home because of the sibs, but I could bring them over there. You two just go ahead."

"What was she talking about?" James asked, after Gypsy spun off on her bike.

"Baby-sitting her sisters . . . Raven and Sasha. With luck, we won't run into them. They're brats."

I felt a little uneasy about going to the mall. It was situated just on the outskirts of town, and lots of kids hung out there, but we never had. I mean, we'd go shopping now and then, but we never went there just to kill time. I can't recall that our folks had told us not to. I guess it was simply understood. Anyway, I decided there was no harm in going over to see what it was like.

Today James had his Nikes tied by the strings around his neck. He put them on and tossed the Rollerblades into my bike basket. We rode over, two on the bike as before.

"Is there a sports store here?" I asked James as we went through the mall entrance. "Where they might have skates? I'd like to scope out the prices."

"Oh, sure. The store's on the next level, toward the other end."

As James and I strolled along I saw a few kids from school. The girls, especially, noticed James. I tried to look cool, as though we were an item. James was happily unaware.

Then he put his hand on my shoulder. "It's there,

see?" And I saw, but mostly *felt*. It was the first time he'd touched me like that.

"Let's go over," I said. And as we walked toward the store, his hand fell away from my shoulder. Darn.

And then I stopped so suddenly I must have vibrated. "Oh, no!"

"What?" James looked toward where I was staring, but all he saw was a girl and a man.

"That's my sister Alice . . . and I don't know who." *Kidnapper* went through my mind. But even as it did, my sensible side said you don't stand around and chat up someone you intend to whisk away for whatever purposes.

"Don't you know the guy?"

"No." He didn't look sinister. In fact he had the fresh, boyish quality that the young partners on TV detective shows have. But that could be to put my sister off guard. "I've got to see what's up," I said. "Protect my sister." I started off.

"Maybe he's a teacher," James said, trailing after me.

"Hello, Alice," I said.

Turning and seeing me, she blushed a deep red. "Oh. What are *you* doing here?"

"It's an open market."

The man smiled at me. He had great teeth and a cleft in his chin. "Are you by any chance one of the sisters?" he asked.

"I'm Emma. Who are you?"

"Em-ma!" Alice rebuked me.

"I'm Baxter Williams, Channel Eight." He took my hand and shook it.

"Hey!" James said. "You do the news!"

"Well, mostly features. And are you one of the brothers? My, I seem to have hit the jackpot."

"No," Alice said. "He's just a . . . friend." She gave me a look.

Baxter immediately lost interest in James. "So, girls . . . and I must say you don't look at all alike . . ."

"Beth and I do, and Craig a little," Alice said. "Drew and Emma are both dark-haired and skinny."

"Thanks," I murmured.

Baxter looked at his digital watch. "I've got to get to the station. Do you think, Alice, that you could set up a meeting for me with the five of you? Now that Emma, here, has seen I'm not an ogre, maybe you girls could convince the others. Then the next step, your parents. If they see you want to do it, they'll go along. Won't they?"

"Mmmm . . . maybe," Alice said. I just tried for a skeptical, narrow-eyed look.

"Well, great to meet you, Emma." Baxter shook my hand again. "And Alice, as always, delightful. And, uh . . . you, too." He didn't bother to get James's name before hurrying away.

"You sneak," I said to Alice after Baxter was out of earshot. "Wait until the folks find out."

"And who's going to tell them?" She knew I wouldn't.

"What?" James was totally baffled.

"Oh . . . this is my sister Alice."

"Hi."

"So you're the mysterious James." Alice dipped her

head a little and dimpled, in a new way she'd developed when she was around guys. "I was wondering if we'd ever get to meet you. My sister is so mysterious."

"Put it on ice, Alice," I said.

"But what was that all about?" James asked. "I mean, it's none of my business, but . . . Channel Eight!"

"He wants to do a feature on us when we graduate this spring."

"You and Emma are both graduating?"

"Along with the other three." Alice rolled her eyes. "Don't tell me she's kept quiet about it all this time."

"I've only known him a couple of weeks," I said. "Three, maybe."

"Quiet about what? I don't get it."

Alice found her reflection in the shop window and fluffed her hair. "Tell him, Emma."

"Well . . . we're . . . my sisters and brothers and I . . ."

"Quints!" Alice all but shouted. "You act like it's something shameful, when you should be proud. We're quintuplets, James, quintuplets!"

"Really?" James looked at us as I knew he would . . . as though we were freaks of nature. "Then you should be . . . like, famous."

"Exactly!" Alice triumphed. "You've got it, and we would be, if our Neanderthal parents didn't keep us under wraps!"

"Alice!"

"Well, it's true. We could be on the cover of . . . of *People*."

"Sure." Tears came to my eyes. I walked away.

James caught up with me. "Hey, Emma, I'm sorry. I didn't mean . . . but it's such a shock. I thought you were . . . well . . ."

"What?"

"A sweet, ordinary girl . . ."

"But now you find out I'm some kind of freak."

"Come on, Emma."

This time his hand didn't feel good on my shoulder. I shrugged it off. "Leave me alone."

"This doesn't . . . I mean, well I'm, well, surprised, but it doesn't really make any difference . . . you know, between us."

But it would change things. I knew it would. James just wouldn't see me the same way from now on, thanks to my sleazy sister.

CHAPTER 12

*D*uring the next week James called a couple of times, but I wouldn't talk to him. *Either he's pretending things are the same,* I thought, *or he wants to hang around in case I turn into a celebrity.*

"You're being incredibly immature," Alice said. "Leaving that poor boy in such a dither. I'm almost tempted to try to cheer him up."

"Be my guest," I said. I didn't think my sister was his type. But then, what did I know?

As for Mr. Baxter TV, I felt sure he was blowing in the wind. He'd never get the okay from my parents, my brothers, or me. Only Beth was on Alice's side. As always.

Nothing at all was said on the parental front, so I knew Alice hadn't said a word. She wasn't stupid.

Dad was all intent on the geography project. Every night when we sat down to dinner, the globe he'd brought home was in the center of the table. "Drew, where are the Greater Antilles?" Dad would bark. "Beth, locate Cape Horn." When he said, "Craig, where are the Canary Islands?" Craig gave Aunt Toots's address.

"You clowns may think this is one huge joke, but someday . . ."

"Honey, do we have to have this every night?" Mom objected.

"Yes, we do. Someone has to take responsibility for these geographic ignoramuses."

"When's Natalie coming to visit?" Beth asked.

"I don't know for sure," Mom said.

My heart gave a little lurch. Every time Natalie was mentioned I was afraid I'd accidentally say something about the wedding.

"Don't change the subject," Dad said to Beth. "Where's the Bering Sea?"

* * *

I practiced my monologue—a scene from *The Glass Menagerie*—in front of a mirror every night. When Saturday came, my bones were like cooked pasta.

"Gypsy, I can't do it," I said as we walked through the laundromat into the drama room. "I'll feel . . . just so stupid, up there in front of all of them."

"That's because you haven't learned the art of detachment," Gypsy said. "It'll come to you." We took seats a little away from the others. "It won't be you, Emma Wentworth, getting up there."

"It will be me, Emma Wentworth, making a fool of myself."

"Listen." Gypsy turned to look me squarely in the eye. "You are not Emma. You are Laura, a poor, shy, crippled girl whose only joy in life is those glass animals. Believe you're that girl, and you'll make us believe it."

Helen came bursting into the room, face glowing, looking as though she'd been racing over the moors with Heathcliff.

"All set, thespians?" she asked. "This is the day that separates the sheep from the goats." She took no notice when a couple of kids went, "Maaaa."

"Now, pretend I'm a director or producer of a show . . ."

"She's big enough to be both," I heard someone mutter.

"I'm going to sit in the back of the room. But first I'll pass out numbers." She walked around, handing them out. "You'll go up when your number's called, and give your name and the title of the selection you've chosen for your audition. I won't comment afterward. All I'll say is, 'Thank you, next.' "

"It sounds kind of scary," Dolores said.

"Of course it is. It's meant to be," Helen said cheerfully. "You have to learn to transcend the fear. That's the first thing you learn about auditions."

"Did you ever audition?" Corliss asked Helen.

"Of course. Even when I was in summer stock back East. Sometimes they assigned roles, but often we'd have to try out for a part we really wanted to play."

"Have you ever been on Broadway?" Henry wanted to know.

"No. I did have some bit parts in TV soaps, but then I got married and moved to the Midwest and that was that. Take my advice. If you want to be a Broadway star, don't let love get in the way. Enough of that. Number one, get on up there."

Henry shuffled up to the front.

"Just a minute," Helen said. "I'm not going to keep interrupting, but I do want to say you have to walk up with confidence. As though you're the hottest actor in the world. Try it again, Henry."

Henry swaggered to the front.

"Well, you could tone it down a little," Helen said. "But go on."

Despite being the first, and a little nervous, Henry wasn't bad as the guy who talked to an imaginary rabbit in *Harvey*. We applauded when he finished the monologue.

"No applause," Helen called out. "You're competitors. You don't want to give anyone else a break."

Gypsy muttered, "It's a cutthroat business, baby."

Corliss was next, doing Blanche's mad scene from *A Streetcar Named Desire*. One of the boys, unseen by Helen, stuck his finger down his throat.

Gypsy chose to play Frankie, a tomboy in the play *Member of the Wedding*. I thought she was good, but probably overacted in the part where the girl grabs a butcher knife and digs a splinter from her foot.

Dolores was next. Miss Paleface, no personality. I was off, thinking of my lines, when suddenly I jerked to attention. She was *good*. I don't mean average, okay good, but really good! As Joan of Arc, she seemed to glow. Her speech actually made my spine tingle.

There was a hush when she finished. She dropped

the stance she'd taken for the role and lagged back to her seat, the same colorless Dolores.

"She's got it," Gypsy whispered to me. "Oh, man, has she got it."

Wouldn't you know I was next? Shaking, I got up in front, gave my name and selection, and tried to focus, but as I said the lines I hardly believed them myself. I couldn't get the weak, lonely quality Laura's voice should have. When it was finally over and I hurried back to my seat, I was glad Helen had said not to applaud for anyone. A quick glance at her face told me nothing.

Gypsy leaned toward me and whispered, "You're getting there." I thought there was a note of pity in her voice.

"I was awful."

"No, you have a certain something. It just takes time."

When everyone had finished, Helen's voice boomed out. "Thank you for coming, everyone. We'll be in touch."

Huh?

She walked to the front of the room. "That's what they say at auditions. They never come out and tell you you're great or terrible. What they do is talk among themselves, and then have callbacks. If you get a callback it means you're under consideration, not that you've snagged the part."

"What do you do at a callback?" Henry asked.

"Whatever they tell you. Usually they'll have you read a side in a script. A side is one character's part.

And after it's all over, they'll say again that they'll let you know."

"I guess I won't hold my breath," Henry said. "If I ever audition, it'll be years from now."

Helen's face lighted up like a Halloween pumpkin. "What a great lead-in line for the announcement I'm about to make!"

We all stared at her.

Still beaming, Helen said, "Here's an inside scoop, kids. They're going to film a movie right in this town, very soon."

"A real movie?" we all gasped.

"As real as a movie ever is. It's a contemporary story that takes place in a suburb like this. And here's the cherry on the hot fudge sundae . . . they're going to need some teenage extras!"

I guess we were all stunned, thinking of what this could mean.

"So you guys, having had some instruction, are good candidates for landing roles. Not speaking parts, probably, but maybe a line or two. If that happens, you can join the actors' union. And that puts you on the way to being a pro."

We sat there with our mouths hanging open.

Helen laughed. "I can see you all hate the idea."

"Would we get our names shown?" Terri asked.

"Probably not. Just your faces." She grew more serious. "Now look, even though you're my students, it's no guarantee you'll be picked for a walk-on. Casting directors always have their own visual images in mind. But I think I can promise you'll be given a try."

"When?" we wanted to know.

"It's anybody's guess. A couple of weeks, a couple of months. Whenever the film company gets everything set up. I'm telling you now so you'll have a good reason to work hard."

When we were out front, after class, I asked Gypsy if she thought either of us had a chance.

"It's all in the throw of the dice," she said. "Like Helen said, it depends on what they're looking for. If it's a Miss Young Teen, pretty and charming, you're in. If it's an offbeat kid character type, I have a chance."

"Maybe they'll want both," I said.

* * *

I didn't tell anyone in the family about the movie that was going to be made in our suburb. Alice and Beth would react by really bleaching their hair, and the boys would laugh and make put-down remarks about girls who think they're about to be discovered.

Mom would be okay, but I could just hear Dad saying, "I thought we'd agreed, no notoriety in this family."

Curled up in my easy chair, a lit book on my lap, I thought of how I could answer Dad. Being famous for just being born and being famous (okay . . . well known) for something you could do well were two different things. I could point out that a real star, like Anjelica Huston, wouldn't say, *Oh, please, I don't want to be in that movie because then people would notice me.*

If I could be in the movie . . . I wouldn't even ask for a speaking part . . . it would mean I was someone who

107

stood out in her own special way. People wouldn't think of me as Emma, the quint, but rather, Emma, the actor.

"Emma!"

I went to my bedroom door and called down, "What, Mom?"

"Natalie wants to talk to you!"

I raced down the stairs. Mom said, " 'Bye, honey," and handed the phone to me.

"So what's happening?" Natalie asked after we'd exchanged hellos.

"Nothing much. When are you coming out?"

"Probably in a couple of weeks."

I glanced around. No sign of Mom. Softly, I said, "When are you going to tell the folks?"

"I already have. About a week ago."

"But I thought—!"

"I know. My plan was to fly out and spring the news on everyone, but I just couldn't wait to tell Jean. Well, both of them."

"Do they know I know?"

"Absolutely not! And I asked them not to tell the others yet. So don't let on. Dad would throw a fit."

I knew I should feel privileged, and I did. But I also felt a bit uneasy about having known before anyone else, and having to pretend I didn't.

"Were Mom and Dad pleased?" I asked.

"Oh, sure. They've always liked Noel."

"I think they were afraid you were going to run off with that motorcycle gang guy you used to know."

"Emma, he didn't ride with a gang. He just had a

leather jacket and a bike. You know how Dad gets carried away."

"Yeah."

"Anyway, Zeke was only an interlude. Nothing serious. So how about you, babe? Any guys in your life?"

"Well, I wrote you about James."

"Yeah. How's it going with him?"

"I haven't talked to him much. Ever since he found out I was a quint."

"That turned him off?"

"I guess it was me. I felt funny after he knew, as though I'd lost my identity."

"Tell me about it." Natalie gave a short laugh. "But you can't let being a quint ruin a relationship."

"You may be right. It may just be in my head. He taught me how to Rollerblade. It's such fun."

"There you go. My advice is, ignore the fact that he knows and go skating with the guy."

"I don't have skates."

"Oh. That does present a problem."

For a fleeting moment I thought of asking Natalie for a loan against the checks I'd undoubtedly get from loving grandparents and other relatives for graduation. But then I thought of all the expenses Natalie would have with her wedding.

"Maybe I'll try to get an advance from Mom," I said. "On my allowance."

"Maybe you could hit up Aunt Toots for a loan," Natalie suggested. "You'd never think so, but she's loaded."

"She spends all her money on birds," I said.

"Oh, yeah, Jean was telling me about that. It sounds as though Aunt Toots has lost it. Well, I guess she's happy."

"Natalie," I said, "have you changed your mind about . . . about what you asked me before?"

"What? Oh! About being my maid of honor? Absolutely not! You're in, kid, whether you like it or not. But don't tell the rest of the brat pack. Even the folks don't know about that part."

"My lips are sealed," I said. But as I said it, a feeling of uneasiness came over me. Why, I didn't know. Or maybe I did know, and refused to think about it.

CHAPTER 13

*I*t had been easy enough to promise Natalie I wouldn't tell, but it put a strain on me. I felt deceitful not letting Mom know I knew. But if I did tell her, and Natalie found out, she'd never again trust me with a secret.

I'd have to pretend, that's all. Maybe my acting classes would come in handy. I went back upstairs and sat around thinking about the wedding and romance and all that, and then found myself thinking about James. Not that we had any kind of romance going. He'd touched me on the shoulder. Twice. But the second time didn't count.

Maybe I should call him. All right, I would. I'd see if he'd changed in his attitude toward me.

Before I could chicken out, I dialed his number.

"Emma!" he said. "How are you?" He seemed so glad to hear from me that all my uncertainties vanished. We talked for a while and then he asked if I wanted to go Rollerblading again.

"Sure," I said, "as soon as I can get my own skates."

Now, why had I said that? How could I get a pair before summer?

After we hung up I thought about my options. Gifts, allowance, a pitifully small amount from babysitting . . . that was about it. I was too young to get even a minimum-wage job at a fast food place . . . and then there was Dad. "Who's going to drive you there?" would be the first thing he'd say.

Come on, Emma, I told myself. *You're not stupid. You can think of a way.* And finally I did! Toots! She must get sick of cleaning out all those cages and hallways. Wouldn't she like a break? To go outside, sit down, and smell something besides bird doo?

I gave her a call. I knew I had to be careful how I made the approach, so she'd know up front this was a business deal.

I started right off with, "Aunt Toots, I really need to make some money, and I was wondering . . ."

"Why, darlin', how much do you need? I can let you have it."

For a moment I was tempted, but I said, "No, that's sweet of you, Toots, but I'd rather work for it. I was wondering if you could use some help in cleaning up after the birds."

"Were you thinking of a steady thing, or one big blitz?"

"I . . . uh . . . it would depend."

"You'd probably rather just do it once or twice because on a daily basis you might get too attached to those birds."

"Yeah, I might." Sure.

"Of course, when some new ones hatch, I could maybe let you have a couple . . ."

"Oh . . . uh . . . we have a dog." *Should I say bird dog? No.*

"Then it would never do. Barking dogs upset birds, at least some of them."

"So, could I come over on Saturday and spend a couple of hours?"

"Why, of course!" Toots exclaimed. "You are just the sweetest soul!"

We left it at that.

* * *

Gypsy thought my plan was a great one. She said she'd come along and help. Free of charge. I told her to wear rubber-soled shoes and to bring a scarf for her hair, rubber gloves, and a surgical mask if she wanted to be a friend to her sinuses.

Acting class that Saturday was better than usual. I guess we were all hyped up over the idea that we could land in the movies. Helen passed out scripts from a play called *The Innocents*. It was about two kids who keep a secret from the grownups.

When it was my turn to read the girl's part, I psyched myself up by thinking of my sister Alice and her secret, the TV reporter Baxter. Helen was back to giving comments, and after I'd finished she said I was pretty convincing. I felt good about that until Dolores got up and read.

Her way of reading the lines gave me goose bumps. Her voice . . . even her looks . . . changed. Everyone was hushed afterward. Helen didn't say a whole lot; she didn't have to. We all knew Dolores really had it.

After class was over, Gypsy and I pretended as we rode our bikes to Toots's that we were already famous movie stars out for a bit of exercise.

"Oh!" Gypsy said at one point. "Try to look ordinary! There's a car full of people who are probably fans!"

"Sorry, Vanessa," I replied, "it's impossible for me to look ordinary. Oh, bother those autograph seekers!"

"Such a bore, Candida, but that's the price one pays for being so incredibly beautiful and talented!"

We stopped short at the entrance to Toots's yard. Kurt's truck was parked out in front.

"Hey, Gypsy!" he called. "Good thing you left the address where you'd be. I got a sudden, rush moving job."

"So?"

"So I brought over these two for you to keep an eye on. Your ma's not off till five." He opened the passenger door. "Scoot, kids. And keep out of trouble."

"*Kurt!*"

"See you!" The girls' feet had barely touched the ground when Kurt roared off.

"Oh, great," Gypsy said. "Like we needed this."

Aunt Toots came out of the house. "Well, what have we here?" she said, smiling broadly.

"This is my friend, Gypsy," I said. "And these are Sasha and Raven."

"Well, aren't we going to have a good time!" Toots took the girls' hands and walked toward the house.

"Maybe the name Raven won her over," Gypsy said to me. "You never know."

Toots led the little girls from room to room and introduced them to all the birds. For once, the kids acted like real children instead of wildcats. I noticed that the six-year-old, Sasha, was already scratching her skinny arms and legs. She probably had an allergy. Well, not my problem.

"Where do we begin, Aunt Toots?" I asked.

"I've got a pile of papers in the living room," she said, "and trash bags for the old, soiled papers. You might as well start there."

"I want to help," Raven said. She stuck out her lower lip and glared, ready for an argument.

"You can help by scramming out of here," Gypsy said. "I mean it."

Raven opened her mouth to bellow. For a little kid of three she had an incredibly large mouth.

"Raven!" Gypsy gave her sister the evil eye. "Don't start."

"Come on, girls," Toots said. "I've got some cookies."

When they were gone I said to Gypsy, "Bird cookies."

"Good. Maybe they'll grow feathers and fly away."

The job was worse than I'd imagined. When I opened a cage, the birds would flutter around, beating their silly wings and yapping, and bits of feathers would fly in my face. And I wasn't crazy about the smell.

Gypsy didn't seem to mind. She actually hummed

and sang as she worked. It made me wonder whether she had a stronger nature than I or was just more used to hardship. Both, most likely.

Toots was in the kitchen with the girls when we dragged out large trash bags filled with the soiled papers.

"I guess recycling is not an option here," Gypsy said. "Where shall we dump these?"

"Oh, just line them up out back." When we'd done that, Toots asked, "Are you two ready for the hallway now or would you like to take a break?"

"I'm for going right on. How about you?" I asked Gypsy. She nodded.

As before, the birds were exercising overhead. Gypsy and I put on our head scarves. We started rolling up the papers together, from one end, but then we noticed it was unwise to leave the bare floor exposed.

"Okay, you roll, I'll follow and lay down fresh papers," Gypsy said.

I had to stop rolling quite often to shove the papers into bags. Otherwise, we'd never have gotten them in.

"Do you feel itchy?" I asked Gypsy.

She sneezed. "Yes."

"Eeeh! I got some on my hand. Oh, gross!" I went to the bathroom to wash it off. Yuk. I reached for a towel and a big red and yellow bird—a parrot, I guess—flew down to the rack.

"Don't give me that beady eye," I said as he looked sideways at me. "I'm not the feathered friend type."

I made sure he was still on the towel rack, then opened the door quickly and closed it after me.

When Gypsy and I lugged the five bags of papers from the hallway out to the back, Toots and the girls were outside.

"We've met all the birds!" Sasha said in her shrill little voice.

"And Sweetie kissed me! On the mouth!" Raven screeched.

"Congratulations," Gypsy said. "You've got real appeal."

"Now, wouldn't you two like to take a break?" Aunt Toots said. "I have some lemonade all ready in the refrigerator."

"Sounds good," Gypsy said. She sneezed.

"Yeah, sounds good. Want me to get it?" I asked.

"No, you two rest on those lounge chairs." She turned to Sasha and Raven. "I'm going to ask you to stay outside, too. Some birds are loose in the kitchen and they might fly out if there's too much coming and going."

"Stay!" Gypsy commanded her sisters as they looked about to protest. "Sit!" They obeyed, but with some grumbling.

The lemonade Toots brought out on a tray, with paper cups, was surprisingly good. It cut the prickly, itchy feeling that had been building up in my throat.

As we drank, Aunt Toots started telling Gypsy all about her escapades with Uncle Horace and the square-dancing crowd. "I guess you get the idea that we weren't as square as some people might think, eh, kiddo?" she said, with a wicked laugh.

"Toots, you're a case, and that's the truth," Gypsy

said. I could see they were two of a kind—a little on the wild side, but nice. I was glad they'd met.

I was lounging, eyes closed, halfway listening to their conversation, when I suddenly became aware of the words "to the bathroom." I opened my eyes and turned just in time to see Sasha disappearing inside the kitchen door. It slammed behind her. Oh, well, she wasn't a baby. I relaxed.

Aunt Toots was saying, "No, let me tell you, the worst of it was they'd waxed that dance floor with . . . what? What is it, Sasha?"

The little girl had come back and was standing in front of Toots. "The bird. He left," she said.

Gypsy sat up. "What bird?"

"The one in the bathroom."

"Child!" Alarm was all over Toots's face. "What happened?"

"I just opened the window so he could see outside. And he left."

"Elwood left? You mean that bird flew out the window?" Toots asked, leaping to her feet.

Sasha shrugged a skinny shoulder. "Yeah."

"Oh, no!" Toots rushed for the house with all of us streaking behind her.

At the door, Gypsy turned to her sisters. "Stay outside! I mean it! *Do it!*" They set up a howl.

"Oh, lordy, it's true, it's true!" Toots lamented, coming out of the bathroom. "Elwood has flown right out of here. Now I'll never get him back! Oh, that poor, sweet parrot, out in the cruel world!"

"Maybe we can catch him," Gypsy said. I looked at her. "Well, it's a thought."

"Oh, you never could, but if you did, I'd give you a million dollars!" She paused. "Well, more or less."

"At least we can look," I said. "Maybe he's right outside."

We left the house. The little girls were huddled in the lounge chairs, sniffling. "Stay right there," Gypsy yelled. "Don't you dare move. And stop that noise," she added, as they began howling.

"Here are a couple of cages," Toots said, staggering up behind us. "Maybe if we set them out somewhere, Elwood will fly inside on his own."

Under her breath Gypsy said, "That'll be the day." But in a hearty way, she said, "Good idea. Let's set one here and one over there. And then we'll go out and beat the bushes."

We walked all through the yard, back as far as the creek, without sighting one red feather. Then we circled around, looking up into the trees. Sasha and Raven joined us.

"Hey . . . I think . . . there . . . isn't that Elwood on that branch way up high?" I called.

Just as Aunt Toots and Gypsy joined me, the bird took off for the next tree.

"It's him, all right, it's my baby!" Toots tweeted. "Oh, get him down, girls!"

"I think I can climb the tree," Gypsy said. "I used to do it all the time. But won't he just fly somewhere else?"

"Well, if you can, I'll stand down below with a cage," I said. "He might come to me."

"Okay." Gypsy shrugged. "We might as well try."

Of course the bird flew, as we knew he would . . . but to the next tree, not to the cage. "Sasha," Gypsy called out, "climb up that tree and chase him over here."

Sasha shimmied a little way up the tree—she was agile as a monkey—and the parrot flew from her tree to Gypsy's. The pattern was repeated over and over. We'd lose sight of the bird and then he'd appear somewhere else.

I felt dizzy from looking up.

"Well, I'm ready to cut bait," Aunt Toots said finally, after almost an hour. "It pains me like anything to say it, but I think that's a gone bird. Come on down out of the trees, Gypsy and Sasha. We're licked, and that's the truth."

"Not quite," I said. "Sssh, everybody. I have a feeling . . . I thought I caught a glimpse of red. It's possible Elwood flew back into the bathroom."

"Oh, lordy, lordy," Aunt Toots said. "I hope your eyes saw right."

"Okay, men," I said. "Here's the plan of attack. You all remain stationary. I will proceed cautiously to the site where the suspect may have been sighted and catch him unawares. In other words, slam the window shut. If he's in there, he's ours."

"Yes, captain, *sir!*" Gypsy answered. We'd both watched that old Goldie Hawn movie where she's in the army.

I crept up—don't ask me why, I'm sure Elwood wasn't looking out the window—slouched beneath the sill, reached my hand up stealthily, and slammed the window shut . . . Kaboom!

"Is he in there, oh, is he in there?" Aunt Toots called out as she hustled toward me.

"I can't see inside." The window wasn't all that clean.

"Then I'll just tippy-toe in and take a peek," Toots said. "If you all wouldn't mind waiting out here?" I nodded and she left.

"Did you really see the parrot?" Gypsy asked as Toots went inside.

"I'm not sure."

"You'd better just pray that bird's back," Gypsy said to Sasha. "And would you stop that scratching? You're making me itch all over."

"Oh, no," I said when Toots came out the door and then leaned against it, fanning herself. "She looks ready to pass out . . . come on, quick!"

We raced to my great-aunt. "Oh, Toots, we'll get you another parrot," I wildly promised. "Take it easy . . . here . . ." I supported her by the arm. "Let's go inside."

"Girls," she said, "you'll never believe what I just saw!"

"He's back!" I exclaimed hopefully.

"That's not the half of it!"

"What? What?" Gypsy and I said together.

Toots took a deep breath and looked at each of us in turn. "There are two of them in there now!"

CHAPTER 14

*T*he mystery wasn't solved until the next day when Aunt Toots called.

"Emma," she said, "like lots of things in life, this has a simple explanation."

"Tell me!"

"Well, first I called the police station, but they didn't seem much interested in a found parrot. So then I went to work and called some pet stores, and bingo! Sure enough, a fellow from just down the road had called in to say his parrot had flown the coop. Isn't it funny that there should be another bird person in my very own neighborhood, and me not knowing a thing about it?"

"Yeah. I'll bet he was happy when you called."

"Happy's not the word for it. He was delirious. The bird is one of those yellow-headed Amazons, and it has a whole lot of sentimental value for him. I told him about you girls capturing it and he insisted on giving you a reward."

"Really? Are you sure?"

"That's what he said. You can pick up the money any time you get a chance."

I called Gypsy with the news that we were about to become rich. She was almost blown away. "You keep it all, though, Emma. Your aunt was nice enough to drive the girls and me home, with the bike. And her parrot wouldn't have been lost in the first place if it hadn't been for Sasha."

"But Gypsy, if Sasha hadn't opened the window, the other bird wouldn't have come in later. So she really helped us get that reward."

"I'm not telling her *that*, after I've already bawled her out. Besides, you gave me half of the clean-up money we earned. And I'm hitting my mom for baby-sitting, so I'll do all right. No, Emma, you're the one who made the capture. The reward is yours."

I didn't argue anymore. Gypsy has a very strong sense of what's fair. Her life is often a battleground and I guess she's made up rules of combat and sticks to them. I wish I could say I'm that noble, but I'm not sure I am.

"It was fun, anyway," Gypsy went on. "I'm crazy about your aunt. She's a trip. Are all your relatives that interesting?"

"No. My grandparents are all quiet and normal, and the same goes for my aunts and uncles. Toots is definitely the showpiece character of the tribe."

"What'll you do with the money?"

"Guess."

"Buy a Mazda Miata?"

"Not quite. But something with wheels. Roller-blades."

"All *right!*"

* * *

The secret about Natalie's wedding preyed on my mind. I was relieved and also excited when Natalie called the folks and said she'd arrive on Saturday for a visit.

I went to acting class because Dad and Mom wanted to go alone to the airport to pick up Natalie. That was good, because then Natalie would tell us quints her news at the same time and all I'd have to do would be to act surprised.

Natalie looked great. I could see why Dad used to call her Sparkles, because she gave off a special radiance —even more so than before—and I knew why. She'd let her hair grow long again, it glistened with reddish gold lights, and her cheeks had a new glow. "You look wonderful," I said as I hugged her.

It wasn't until after lunch that Natalie told us the news. I needn't have worried about looking surprised —no one noticed me in the bedlam. Alice and Beth squealed and the boys shouted, "All right!" They were both wild about Noel because he'd always acted like a big brother around them and had promised to take them camping someday in Canada.

We all went out to dinner that night, to the restaurant that had always been Natalie's favorite.

"You remembered!" Natalie said to Dad.

"I remember everything about you."

In that moment, with the sudden, tender look Dad was giving Natalie, I felt for the first time how wrenching it must have been for him when his eldest decided to go live with her mother. Selfishly, I guess, I'd assumed that the five of us more than compensated for the loss of one.

Anyway, it was a great meal, and Dad couldn't have been more mellow. He barely glanced at the bill before hauling out his Visa card.

When we got home we sat around, talking about things in general, and then Natalie asked if we'd mind if she talked to the folks alone.

My heart started pounding. I didn't dare look at Natalie. I was pretty sure that the time had come for her to make the pitch about me being the maid of honor.

I headed for my room, but the boys just naturally went to Alice and Beth's room and it would have looked strange if I didn't join them.

"It's going to be kind of awkward, isn't it?" Beth started out.

"What?" Drew wanted to know.

"Two mothers of the bride." When the boys just stared at her, she said, "Our mom and her real mom, you morons. I mean, will they all sit together in the church, or will Dad sit next to our mom or to his first wife?"

"Maybe he can run back and forth," Craig said.

"My friend Kathy had a wedding like that in her family," Beth said. "The father sat with his present wife, not the one he'd divorced."

"I wonder if they'll get married here or in Colorado,"

I said, just to be saying something. And I really didn't know.

"Why would they get married here when Natalie lives out there, you twit?" Craig said. "I guess we'll all get to go." Then he got a look of pain. "Would we have to get dressed up?"

"That's right!" Alice couldn't have looked happier. "We'll have to get some great new outfits!" And then she gave a gasp.

"What?" Beth asked.

"What if . . . what if Natalie asks us to be in the *wedding party?* Bridesmaids!"

My heart lurched as the two girls squealed, hugged each other, and carried on. I could feel little beads of sweat on my upper lip.

"Knock it off," Drew said to the two of them. "You know Dad wouldn't let us all stand up there in front of everybody."

The girls stopped their commotion to stare at him, wide-eyed. "And why not, pray?" Beth asked.

"Because of the publicity, pray," Craig said. "In fact, I wouldn't put it past him to not even let us go." And then, possibly because the stricken looks on his sisters' faces got to him, he added a bit lamely, "Or we'd have to scatter out and be with other relatives, other adults, so no one would catch on."

Beth looked at him for a moment and then burst into tears.

Alice's face turned pink with anger. "I am just so sick of being treated like . . ."

"Freaks?" Drew helped out.

"No—like some kind of deep, dark secret the family's ashamed of!"

"Chill out, Alice," Craig said. "No one's ashamed. They just want us to have normal lives."

"Well, being quints is normal for us!"

"It's other people, Alice," I said. "If they'd just leave us alone."

"Oh, leave, yourself," Alice said. "Get out of my room, all of you. I don't want to be around people who are ashamed of being related to me. You can stay, Beth."

"Thanks." Beth gave us a look that said, *What else? It's my room, too.*

Just then we heard raised voices from downstairs. Craig opened the door just in time for us to hear Dad shout, "Absolutely no, Natalie! I won't allow it!"

"You don't have that much to say about it!" Natalie shouted back. "It's my wedding!"

"Well, I'm not going to let you do this and create a rift in the family."

"Great. You want to run this like you run everything else!"

Our mom broke in. "Natalie, honey—"

"All right, Dad." Natalie's voice was still loud but she'd stopped shouting. "I'll give up on the idea. But I'll also give up on the idea of a big wedding. And later on when you're feeling sorry for yourself, just remember, you're the cause of it, not me."

Craig turned to face all of us. "What did I tell you?"

With a sob, Alice shouted, "I said to get out of here!"

The boys and I left.

I threw myself on my bed. Oh, why did everything always go so wrong? Why couldn't I have been born into an average family like everyone else I knew? No one else had this problem!

Also, I felt guilty. Guilty about not telling Alice and everyone that Natalie wanted just me in her wedding, and guilty for going along with it when Natalie first asked. I should have realized it wouldn't work out.

I lay there trembling as the voices continued downstairs. In a little while Dad would storm up into my room and accuse me of scheming with Natalie behind his back, and . . . and . . . I didn't know what, after that.

Time passed. I rose up on an elbow and listened. I couldn't hear a sound, so I slipped over to the door and eased it open. Quiet down there. That was strange. Then I could tell that my parents were coming up the stairs. Where was Natalie?

I eased the door shut, went over to my desk, and turned on the light, as though I'd been studying all this time. Sure, on a Saturday night. Good move, Emma.

Dad and Mom didn't knock on the door, though. After a while I knew they weren't going to. I waited and waited, wondering if my half-sister would come up to see me. Finally I sneaked downstairs. I looked in the living room, the kitchen, and the family room with its fold-out sofa. Natalie wasn't there.

Where was she?

Had the row been so awful that she'd just picked up and gone back to Colorado? Her carry-on wasn't there.

I felt hollow. And at the same time heavy, as though my bones couldn't make me move.

Dad had really done it this time. Why couldn't he, just for once, let Natalie do things the way she would if she had a normal family? It wasn't her fault that her brothers and sisters had been born in a bunch. Being the sister of quints was almost as bad as being one herself. It was no wonder she'd moved away to live with her mom.

CHAPTER 15

I hated to go down for breakfast the next morning, but at the same time I didn't want to call attention to myself. I timed it so I went down with Alice and Beth.

"Where's Natalie?" one of them asked.

Mom was busy pouring orange juice. "She went over to a girlfriend's house to spend the night."

"How come?" I asked.

Dad looked up from the Sunday business section of the paper. "Because she wanted to. Sit down and eat."

"When's she coming back?" Drew asked, pulling out his chair.

Mom spilled a little juice. "Well . . . whenever."

Everyone could sense the strain, but no one wanted to call attention to it and thus draw fire. The meal was not one you'd file away as a great occasion.

Just before noon Natalie returned. She looked pale and her eyes were a little swollen. The radiance was gone.

"Hi, honey," Mom said, putting her arms around Natalie. "You're just in time for lunch."

"No, thanks. Claudia and I had a late breakfast."

"Hi, Natalie," Dad said.

"Hi." She looked around at the rest of us, gave us a weak smile, and asked the boys about sports. We all knew that wasn't what was on her mind, but it gave her a little time to get together what she had to say.

Finally it came out. "I've decided to forget about a big wedding and have a very simple one instead. Just a few friends out in Colorado."

No one said a word. We all kind of froze, staring at Natalie.

She swallowed. "It's the best thing. That way there'll be no feelings hurt . . . no . . . conflict."

"Oh, but sweetheart," Mom protested. "You shouldn't . . ."

"It's okay. It'll work out. I'll let you know more later."

"I think we should all go sit down and calmly discuss this," Dad said. "Surely something . . ."

"It's all settled. I'll keep you informed. If not before the wedding, then after." Her words came out like slivers of ice.

Natalie hugged each of us kids in turn. "I'm sorry we didn't have a chance to catch up on things, but maybe sometime . . ."

She went to Mom and put her arms around her. " 'Bye, Jean."

"What's this ' 'bye' business?" Dad said. "Where are you going?"

"Back. Claudia's out in the car waiting for me."

"Natalie! You can't . . . !"

"Dad, give it up," Natalie said. "I'm leaving. Now."
And she did.

Dad sagged as though he'd been punched out. He gave Mom a stricken look, then turned and went upstairs. I'm not sure, but I think he was crying. I'd never known he could.

"Mom . . ." Alice said. "What happened?"

"Later." Mom turned and went upstairs, too.

My brothers and sisters and I just stood there looking at one another.

"I've never seen Natalie like that before," Drew said. "So riled up."

"That was last night," Alice said. "Now she just acted hurt. I wonder what went on last night, besides what we heard."

"I wonder if she really meant what she said, about having a small wedding. Doesn't she want any of us there?" Beth asked. "It would break Dad's heart. And Mom's. And mine."

Craig gave Beth a steady look. "Don't be so dramatic," he said. "This'll all blow over. Just wait and see." And to Drew, "Let's go out and shoot a few baskets."

After they left, Alice and Beth said they were leaving this house of gloom and going to a girlfriend's. They asked if I wanted to go along but I said no.

After they left I wandered around the house feeling miserable. I ended up in the family room.

Thinking that looking at photos of happier times might cheer me up, I got out old family photograph albums. They made me feel sad instead. Especially the shots of us at a picnic when Natalie was home one summer. In one photo Dad and Natalie mugged for the camera, arms around each other's neck and looking so funny and happy. Would we all ever be together like that again?

Finally I went up to my room, hoping I could lose myself in a book. But I kept seeing Dad's face when his eldest daughter told him she was leaving. Would she ever come back?

I couldn't even cry. I just sat huddled in my chair, feeling worse by the minute. It was my fault, this whole misunderstanding. After all, Dad must have meant me when he said to Natalie, "I'm not going to let you do this and create a rift in the family."

Being Natalie's maid of honor *would* create a rift. I could see that now. Probably the boys wouldn't mind, but Alice and Beth would really feel hurt and left out. Why hadn't I seen that? I guess I was so thrilled at having been chosen that I didn't even think about the others.

Natalie, too, should have known better. But love probably does that to you . . . makes you blind about other things.

So now the situation was about as bad as it could get. It looked as though none of us would get to go to the wedding. At the moment, Dad blamed Natalie. I didn't think he knew that I was in on it, that I'd agreed to be maid of honor. Did I have the courage to tell him?

And what about my brothers and sisters? How would they feel toward me when they found out? Would they hate me forever?

There was a scratching at my door. Sylvester. I let him in. Sitting on the floor and wrapping my arms around the dog's shaggy body, I thought that here was the only member of the family who wouldn't look down on me in the future. Sylvester's fur was damp. He'd been outside frisking around with the boys, but had had sense enough to come inside when it started to drizzle. I could still hear the *whomp* of the basketball outside.

What a gray day. And as I dragged around my room I could picture the many dreary days ahead, even if the sun did shine.

Finally I knew that I'd never get through today unless I did what I dreaded to do . . . have a face-off with Dad. He'd be horrible, but nothing he might say could make me feel any worse than I did right now.

Taking several deep breaths, I went down the hall and knocked on his and Mom's bedroom door.

"Yes?"

"It's Emma. Okay if I come in?" For a moment I hoped they'd tell me to go away.

Mom opened the door. She looked pale and tired instead of upbeat, the way she usually does.

"Come on in," Dad invited. He was stretched out on the bed, hands behind his head. He looked battle worn. "Sit down, Emma."

Mom touched my shoulder and steered me toward the yellow floral chaise. We both sat down facing Dad.

"You have something to say?" Dad didn't look at me. He wasn't going to make this easy.

"It's about Natalie's wedding." Silence. "I know what . . . what she told you."

"And what was that?"

"That she wanted me to be her maid of honor."

Now Dad turned his head on the pillow to look at me. "Oh, you knew that, did you?"

I was afraid he was going to ask how long I'd known, and I'd be sunk. But instead he said, "And how did you feel about that?"

"I was pleased, but . . ." My voice faltered. "I guess it wouldn't be fair to the others."

"You're damn . . . you're darn right it wouldn't. If you can see that, why can't Natalie?"

He was beginning to get steamed. I wanted to defend Natalie, but at the same time I wasn't anxious for a full-blown outburst.

"Honey." Mom came to the rescue. "It is Natalie's wedding, and she has the right—"

"She doesn't have the right to single out one of the kids and let the others feel left out!" Dad jumped up and slapped at his pockets. He'd given up smoking months ago, but in times of stress he still reached for a cigarette.

"Maybe she could have all of us?" I said in a small voice.

"Don't think I didn't suggest that. And you know what she said? Tell her, Jean."

"Oh, Jack, try to calm down." Mom reached over and smoothed my hair down my back.

"I'll tell you!" Dad had begun pacing. "She said she

wasn't going to have her wedding turned into a damned circus!''

"Not in those exact words," Mom said.

"All her life, ever since you quints were born, Natalie's had this thing about the attention you get. Well, I could understand that when she was young. But she's a grown woman now. It's time she got her act together!"

"What'll happen?" I asked in a trembly voice.

"What?" Dad whirled around to face me. "She'll go ahead and get married, but we won't be there!"

"Oh, Dad!" Now I started to cry. "That would be awful."

"It's her choice." Dad walked out of the room.

I crumpled up against Mom. I was crying hard, and I could hear her sniffling, too. "Could you talk to Natalie's mother? You two always got along. Maybe . . ."

"Honey, I don't know what I'd tell her. Natalie's her daughter. I can't interfere."

"Then what can we do? It would be terrible if Dad didn't go!"

"I can't see any solution. You know, they're two of a kind, your father and Natalie. Both so strong-willed . . . like a pair of antelopes with locked horns."

"Mmmm." I blew my nose. Then I had an idea. "What if I told the rest of them about Natalie wanting me . . . you know . . . and they said they didn't care? Would that help?"

"I don't know." Mom got up and looked out the window. "I know the boys wouldn't mind one bit, but Alice and Beth?"

"Yeah, you're right." I couldn't see them taking it well.

"It's gone too far, anyway," Mom said, turning away from the window. "Your father would never back down."

"Right again." I lay down on the chaise sideways, my head cushioned on my arm. "Why does everything have to be so complicated? Why can't we just be happy?"

"We can be, but not always. If we were happy all the time, wouldn't that get boring?"

"I could handle it."

Mom went into the bathroom and splashed water on her face. When she came back she'd put on lipstick and brushed her hair.

"Let's go downstairs," she said. "I guess everyone's forgotten about lunch."

"Mommmmmm!" came a bellow from downstairs.

"I guess not everyone," Mom said. She held out her hand. "Come on, sweetie. Let's go down and feed the troops. What's left of them."

When we sat down to eat, Dad asked where the other girls were.

"The tarts?" Craig asked.

"Don't refer to your sisters in that way!" Dad said.

Craig and Drew exchanged looks.

"Our esteemed sisters are at their girlfriend's house," Craig said. "Stupid Samantha's."

"Why can't they ever hang around here?" Dad asked. "What's a family for?" When no one came up with a reply, he went on, "Families should stick together."

I'm sure the boys were thinking, *How about you and Natalie?* I know I was.

I was also thinking that I would have to tell Alice, Beth, Craig, and Drew the reason behind the falling out. It would be hard. I would have to make them understand how private Natalie wanted her wedding to be. It was her day, after all. Yet she wanted someone from the family to be in the wedding party.

"But why you, Emma?" each of my sisters would ask. "Why not me?"

What answer could I give them?

I'd wait a while before telling. Maybe, in that time, I'd think of the right thing to say.

CHAPTER 16

I guess even after a death in the family, life goes on. Of course, our situation wasn't that traumatic . . . far from it. But it did feel like something close to us had died. There was that little space that hadn't been there before.

One night I called Natalie and told her how sorry I was about what had happened. "It's probably my fault," I said.

"No, it's not. It's Dad's. If he hadn't made an issue about your being maid of honor, everything would be fine. Now no one will be there. Serves him right."

For a while after that call I felt bad all over again. But there was so much going on right then that the Natalie-Dad feud began to fade from my mind.

Graduation was now only five weeks away. Finals loomed.

All five of us were good students, and competition kept even the laggers (Alice and Craig) on the mark. There was no letting down now, with eighth grade diplomas a must.

But it wasn't all school.

Thanks to Toots and her birds, I was able to get the Rollerblades, and knee guards and a helmet, too. The parrot man, Mr. Horton, had insisted on personally presenting me with the reward.

"It's too much!" I'd gasped as he handed over a crisp one-hundred-dollar bill.

"Nonsense," he'd said. "That parrot is priceless, at least to me! And don't forget I got a reward, too. I met this charming lady."

"Oh, go on." Toots blushed and gave him a nudge with her elbow. Then she'd made *me* blush by asking, "How's that sweetie of yours, Emma?"

"He's okay," I'd told her. "But he's just a friend, you know."

James and I were now talking on the phone like before, and once he'd even come over to the house to pick me up to go skating. I was really scared that first time Dad met him, but Dad didn't make a fuss. I guess the fight with Natalie had chilled him out. My sisters thought James was "the very cutest" and Craig said, "Yeah, he's all right." Drew said he was cool.

When I practiced Rollerblading at home, Drew often hung around. He was perishing to skate himself, but he couldn't squeeze into my shoes. Finally, though a miser to the core, he used some of his considerable savings (considerable compared to the amounts the rest of us had stowed away) to buy a pair.

"Would you or James mind if I hung out with you tomorrow?" he asked me one Friday night as we were going up the stairs to our rooms.

"Why should either of us mind?"

"Well . . ." Drew made little kissing sounds.

"Oh, please."

"I wouldn't be a third wheel? Or in this case, blade?"

"Drew . . . all we do is skate around. It's not a big nationally televised event."

My brother glanced over his shoulder. "Speaking of television . . . have you heard any more from that news guy, Baxter?" I'd told him about the meeting at the mall.

"Not a word. Do you think maybe Alice has given him the brush?"

Drew gave a short laugh. "Not possible. Not Alice."

"Then I wonder what's next. Baxter said something about getting together with all five of us, but so far nothing's happened."

"With all the prime news stuff going on he's probably lost interest," Drew said. "That's fine with me."

"Me, too."

It was ironic (if that's the word) that the very next Monday night Baxter materialized on our doorstep.

All of us, except Mom and Alice, were in the family room, watching a TV sitcom. Mom came to the doorway and motioned for Dad to turn down the sound.

He did, and we all looked around, impatient, because they were just getting to the best part of the show.

"There's someone here who wants to see you," Mom said.

"Tell him we don't need insurance or a new religion or kitchen improvements," Dad said, beefing up the sound.

"Jack . . ."

"What?" He lowered the sound just a little.

"It's someone from a TV station. He wants to talk to us . . . all of us."

Dad hit the wrong button and the TV blared. He turned it off completely then and stood up. "He must want to exploit us in some way. I'll throw him out, the scum."

"Daddy . . ." Alice had come to the doorway. "Please don't make a scene and get arrested."

Dad pushed her aside and stalked out of the room. Alice gave us a pleading look which said *Don't tell*. As though we would.

We edged into the front hall as Baxter was saying, "Please, could we just sit down and talk?" Mom motioned toward the living room while Dad glared.

The five of us kids drifted into the room but stayed near the door.

Baxter, who had seated himself, looked very much at ease. I wondered if his training before the cameras had taught him coolness in the face of the enemy. Mom sat down, too, and Dad reluctantly followed suit.

"Who are you?" Dad asked. Just like that. *Who are you?*

If Baxter felt a little insulted that he wasn't instantly recognized, he didn't show it. "Baxter Williams, a newscaster on Channel Eight," he said. "Features, mostly."

"And what brings you here?" Dad always got right to the point.

"The station is interested in doing a segment on the

graduation of the Wentworth quintuplets," Baxter said. It was then he appeared to notice us for the first time, hovering in the doorway. "And I take it these are the famous five?" He broke into a big, professional-type smile. His teeth had probably been bonded, they looked so perfect. I wondered if Alice would get the name of his dentist for the tiny little space between her two front teeth.

She now stepped forward, hand extended. "I'm Alice," she said.

"Well, hello, Alice." Baxter stood up, as though he was meeting a royal personage for the first time, and shook her hand. "And you?" He looked at Beth.

"I'm Beth . . ." More shaking of hands. "And this is Emma."

"Beth, Emma, hello. And now which boy is which?"

"Craig." Another handshake.

"Drew." Ditto.

"What a great-looking bunch of kids," Baxter said to Dad and Mom as he sat down again. "You must be ever so proud."

"All right, you've met them." Dad looked at his watch as though he had to catch a plane. "And that's it. That's as far as it goes."

"But look . . ." Baxter, elbows on knees, leaned forward. "They're wonderful kids. They made news when they were born. Now they're about to graduate. The world wants to see them again, see how they've developed."

"Then the world can go take a hike. It's nobody's business how they've developed."

Alice was twisting her lips, dying to jump into the conversation, but she had to keep her cover. She glanced at me, but then her gaze fixed on Beth.

Beth, the stooge, responded. "Dad, I think it would be . . ."

"I'm not interested in what you think."

I wanted to speak up and say I was against the idea, but I knew Alice and Beth would never forgive me if I did. And anyway, Dad was handling it.

Mom, her smile trying to make up for Dad's rudeness, said, "Mr. Williams, please understand our position. We want the children to grow up naturally and not be made to feel unusual in any way. We want people to think of them only as five brothers and sisters . . . individuals."

"Which I certainly can understand," Baxter said, now furrowing his brow a little, trying for sincerity. "But I want to assure you, we don't wish to put them in the spotlight . . ."

"Just on the ten o'clock news, with murderers and rapists."

"Daddy!" Beth objected.

"No dice," Dad said, getting up. "It's been nice meeting you, Mr. . . ."

"Baxter Williams, Channel Eight."

". . . Mr. Channel Eight," Dad said. "You can go back and tell your bosses that I'm a . . ."

"Grouchy old grinch," Alice said under her breath.

". . . A stick-in-the-mud who believes in the sanctity of the home and family."

"Give me strength," Beth said.

"Well, I can certainly understand that." Baxter looked sorry when he stood up, but then his smile flashed as he held out his hand toward Dad. Dad reluctantly shook it. Then Baxter shook hands with Mom and with each of us in turn.

"Please take my card," he said, pulling one out of his pocket. Dad made no move, so Mom reached out for it.

"Could I have one?" Craig asked. He took it as Dad gave him a look. "Just to show the guys. To prove I met a real TV celebrity."

Baxter gave a laugh he must have learned at announcer school. "Craig, I'm not a celebrity. Just your ordinary working stiff." He handed out cards to all of us. "It was a pleasure to meet each one of you."

As Mom walked him to the door, he said, "If you should change your mind, you know where to reach me."

When she came back, she said, "Jack, you might have been a little more gracious."

"What? And encourage him? Those guys are like buzzards. They just keep circling overhead unless you hit 'em with buckshot."

"Actually," Alice said, "what's so bad about being famous?"

Dad gave her a steady look. "If you're famous for swimming the English Channel or inventing a new vaccine, that's one thing. To get your mug on television just for being who you are means nothing. I've only contempt for people like that."

"What a surprise," Drew mumbled to me as we walked out together.

Later on, I stopped in the middle of homework to wonder if Dad would consider acting a just cause for fame. He might. But did I have enough talent to become a good actor? Sometimes I thought I did well in class and sometimes I felt like a blob.

Soon, now, I'd find out how well I measured up. Helen had told us the movie auditions were coming up in a little while. I shook inside thinking of how scary it would be to stand in front of real professional directors. Helen had said it was part of the game . . . something you had to stiffen your back and do.

"If you're rejected, you can't take it personally," she'd said. "All it means is you're not the right type for that particular part. So then you just go out and audition some more."

Right. As though movies were being made every month in our suburb. If I got a part, no matter how small, I'd be Emma Wentworth, the actor. If not, I'd just be Emma Wentworth, the quint. It was as simple as that. Or so I thought that night.

CHAPTER 17

I could feel my youth slipping by. That may sound strange, coming from a thirteen-year-old, but you know what I mean. I would never be a grammar school kid again. Next year I'd be in high school, and before I knew it I'd be an adult.

And now, it seemed that just because I wanted to savor these last few weeks of being really young, they slipped away, spun themselves into the past. Suddenly graduation day was here.

Because there were two junior highs, the graduation ceremonies were staggered. Beth's and mine was on Friday. James said he couldn't come to my ceremony because of family plans. I knew I'd be at his, though, because he would graduate on Thursday night, the same as Alice, Craig, and Drew.

There was nothing anyone (meaning Dad) could do that Thursday about three of his kids striding one after the other across the stage to receive diplomas. But if he was worried about any special attention, he needn't have been. The shouts and whistles for my siblings were no more than those for anyone else. Lots of fond relatives ran down the aisles to snap pictures of their darlings, and the whir of camcorders was like the sound of crickets.

"Why are these people acting like a bunch of idiots?" I heard Dad say to Mom. I think the people in front of us heard, too, but they didn't turn around.

"Honey, they're proud of their kids," Mom said, clutching Dad's arm. "I think it's sweet."

"I don't," Dad said. "I think it's pathetic."

I guess he meant the public display, because earlier, at home, he'd been the one who kept wanting more pictures. He had to have shots of each of us alone, each of us with him and Mom, the girls alone, the boys alone, and so forth.

I knew Beth had her camera in her purse at that very moment and was itching to jump up and grab a few shots of Alice, Craig, and Drew, but she had sense enough not to cause a scene with Dad. I wanted so much to borrow the camera to catch a shot of James, but I didn't dare.

Dad had agreed to take all of us to a new ice cream place afterward. When we got there it seemed half the graduating class had had the same idea. I looked around for James but didn't see him. Dad was in a good mood. He was even a good sport about standing in line while we waited for a table.

"Do we have to do this again tomorrow night?" he asked me, his arm draped over my shoulder.

"No. Of course I'll feel discriminated against forever,

but that's all right." I smiled up at him as he gave my shoulder a little shake.

Alice was flitting all over the place. She seemed to know everyone in her graduating class and she also seemed to be everybody's favorite. How did she ever get to be so self-assured?

Beth watched Alice but didn't make a move to join her. In this situation, she was closer to me. "Tomorrow night's our turn," she said. "Let's go somewhere else. This place is too noisy."

As it turned out, we didn't go back to that same place, but not because of the noise. Just before we left for the grade school the next night, our neighbor, Mrs. Burke, stopped by. "I wondered if you saw this," she said.

"Why?" Mom reached out for the evening paper. "What's happened?"

"Nothing bad. It's a write-up about your kids."

Mom gave a little groan. Dad was already out at the car and so were the boys. "Let's see." She opened the paper and Alice and Beth and I crowded around.

The heading said LOCAL QUINTS GROW UP AND GRADUATE. There was a group shot of us when we were a year old and then single school photos, taken this year. And then there was a candid shot of us taken just last night, when we were standing in a bunch by the car—before leaving for the ice cream place.

"Someone must have had a long-range photo lens," Beth said. "Now I know how Princess Di feels."

"But at least you weren't wearing a bikini," Alice said. "I hate this. My hair looks awful."

"You want the paper?" Mrs. Burke asked. "I can get another one."

"We subscribe. It just happened that no one's read it yet." Mom gave a little smile. "I'll forget to mention the article to Jack until later."

"Someone's going to spill the oats," Alice said as we went out the front door. "Count on it."

"Well, don't you be the one to spill," Mom murmured. "Let's just get through the ceremony, and then . . ."

When Beth and I went to the front of the auditorium I waved to Gypsy, seated several rows ahead of me. She gave the thumbs-up sign that meant her mom had broken down and given her Rollerblades for graduation. Earlier today, on the phone, Gypsy had said she had to go out afterward with her mom and Kurt and the two sisters, who would probably ruin the evening.

Aunt Toots was at the ceremony with Mr. Horton, the parrot man. They'd come both nights, and we'd invited them to join us afterward. "Thanks, but I can't take the noise," Aunt Toots had said. "Bird racket I'm used to, but not all that chirping of the kids. We're cutting out right after you chickens get your papers."

As they had last night, one row of kids at a time went up for their diplomas. As we were standing in line waiting to go up the steps to the stage, a kid named Josh turned and said, "Hey, Wentworth wimps, are you getting gold medals tonight for being so famous and everything?"

"Are you getting one for being the biggest scuzzball?" Beth retorted.

"I just *loved* your baby picture," Josh went on. "You still look like an infant, drool-face." He gave a yelp as the kid behind him hit him in the back. Josh stumbled up the stairs but managed to get his balance before walking across the stage.

"I could just die," Beth whispered to me. "I feel like everyone's talking about us."

"Don't worry. They're only interested in their own kids," I said.

Beth walked across to the usual applause, and I followed, feeling as if I were in a dream. Then we were back in our seats, clutching our diplomas, proof that we'd weathered eight years of school.

The first alert Dad had, I guess, that tonight was a little different from last night came when we were gathered together afterward at the back of the auditorium. First it was just little clutches of people staring at us while we chattered away. Some even pointed. Then a bold mother sneaked up and snapped a picture of us. Before we could react, others did the same.

"Let's get out of here," Dad said angrily. "What's wrong with people, anyway? Why do they have to act like such fools?"

We headed for the car. Someone called out, "There they are, the quints!" My brother Craig yelled something quite rude and unprintable and Mom told him to cool it. Now everyone seemed to be aiming a camera at us. Some probably didn't even know why. I felt a little blinded by the flashes.

I have to give it to Dad. He could have taken us straight home, but instead he drove several miles to a place he liked near the airport that had fabulous desserts. No one there paid the least bit of attention to us. We managed to have a good time, but still, I missed being with my classmates, especially Gypsy. And now, instead of feeling a little sad about my fleeting childhood, I began wishing I were already grown up and gone.

Beth gave a sigh as she spooned up chocolate mousse from a bowl made of chocolate. "I wish Natalie could've come for our graduations. It didn't seem right not to have her here."

"She has a job," Drew pointed out. "When you're pulling down a salary you can't just buzz off whenever you feel like it."

"We didn't go to her graduation," Craig observed.

"Brilliant. We were babies," I said.

"It looks like we won't even go to her wedding," Alice said, not looking at Dad. "It'll probably break her heart."

"How about if we went in disguise?" Craig suggested. "Like . . . like . . ." He shrugged. "Well, you get the idea."

After an unusual silence Dad said, "I guess I should talk to Natalie. I owe her an apology."

It's too bad someone didn't snap our picture at that moment. The photographer would have caught us all with mouths open, dessert spoons suspended in space.

Dad went on. "What I'm saying is, I can understand what Natalie meant about a circus, after the way people acted tonight."

"I felt like busting their cameras," Craig said.

"Oh, please." Alice rolled her eyes. "You're not exactly one of those movie jocks who bash the press. You're just an itty-bitty freak of nature. Ouch!" she yelled as Craig punched her arm.

"Cut the capers," Mom said. "You're young adults now."

"Yeah, you big fat jerk," Alice said to Craig.

"Speaking of cameras," Dad said, "I wish we had one now. It'd be nice to have a group shot of us here, celebrating."

With a big smile, Beth opened her purse. "Ta da!" she sang out, holding up the camera.

A waiter obligingly took several shots. He didn't seem to think it strange that there were five of us the same age. Since we were near the airport, he might have thought we were just a group of friends and a pair of unlucky parents on the way to some vacation spot.

"At least that Channel Eight guy had the decency to back off," Dad said. "No TV coverage. Sometimes it pays to use a little muscle."

We gave each other sideways looks. What Dad had used was rudeness, not muscle.

"Stand by your principles," Dad went on. "Remember that, kids. Don't give in to what you know is wrong just because someone asks you to."

Under her breath Alice said, "There's nothing *wrong* about being on TV." I'm sure Dad heard but he pretended not to.

He was on a roll. "Actually, except for a few misguided parents with their cameras, we managed to pull off two graduations. And there was no press butting in and spoiling everything."

Craig cleared his throat. Then he shifted a little, pulled a piece of folded newspaper from his pocket, and handed it to Dad.

"What's this?" he asked, while a resigned look came over Mom's face.

Dad unfolded the page and stared at the headline and our pictures. "Where'd you get this?" he asked Craig.

"A kid gave it to me . . . Phil Lewis. It was in tonight's paper."

I guess everyone expected Dad to crumple up the clipping and say something like, *Heads are going to roll for this!* I know that's what I thought he would do.

But his face didn't flush, and he remained expressionless as he slowly read the article. No one said a word while we watched him; we were too surprised.

When he finished, he turned to us. I thought he looked a little sad. "Kids," he said, "we're going to have to face reality."

Beth licked her lips. Softly she asked, "What do you mean, Dad?"

"The reality is that you kids are different. Not in any way that's important or that you're responsible for."

"We're different," I objected, "because *everyone* is different."

"I know that, babe, and so does anyone with any logic. But the world loves to focus on the unusual. The

154

fact that you guys were born quintuplets qualifies you as unusual."

He sighed and leaned his elbows on the table. "I . . . your mother and I . . . tried to protect you all these years from being exploited. For the most part, I think we succeeded pretty well."

Mom nodded. "You'll never know all the promotions we turned down . . . from cereal to look-alike toys to a line of kids' clothing . . . you name it." She noticed Alice's look of dismay. "It would have meant money and notoriety, sure. But our lives wouldn't have been our own. Everything you did . . . and said . . . would have belonged to the mass market."

"Famous, though," Alice said with a sigh.

Dad waited until the waiter had removed the empty dessert dishes and mopped up the dribbles of bubble gum ice cream, strawberry sauce, and chocolate topping. "Kids," he said, "your mom and I aren't going to be able to protect you from now on."

I felt alarmed. I could hear the others catch their breaths.

"You're not gonna, like . . . ?" Craig asked, round-eyed.

"No." Dad laughed. "We're not going to kick off, if that's what you think. What I mean is . . ." He looked at Mom.

"You'll all be in the same school next year," she said. "There's nothing we can do about that."

"And some kids will notice," Dad said, "and some teachers will notice, and some of them will remark about your being quintuplets. So what'll you do?"

"Punch them out?" Craig looked hopeful. Alice hit him with her elbow from one side and Beth did the same from the other.

"You're going to have to deal with it." Dad looked us each in the eye.

"How're we supposed to do that?" I asked.

"What if kids won't leave us alone?" Beth asked.

"You'll just have to figure out a way," Dad said. For a brief moment a lost look flickered over his face. I suddenly realized that our being quints must not have been easy for Dad either. Our restrictions had also been his.

"Hey," Mom said, "let's lighten up. Does anyone want another round of dessert?"

Practically all of us made barfing noises. Even Craig, who usually is the bottomless pit. But, after all, he had ordered the Pig-Out Perfection, a sickening mass of seven flavors with umpteen toppings.

We headed for home.

As we walked in the back door, the phone was ringing. Every one of us froze. I guess we were thinking, *It's someone from the news media.* I know I was.

Instead, it was Natalie. Sweet Natalie, calling to congratulate each of us on our graduation. She sounded like she usually does . . . kidding around and still being the big half-sister.

When she got through talking to us, she talked to Jean. And then she asked to talk to Dad. I wanted to hang around to hear what he said. As far as I knew, this was the first time they'd talked since she stormed out that day. Were they making up?

Mom noticed me lurking about and made me go upstairs with the others, so I couldn't tell how things were
going between Natalie and Dad.

I had another concern. Had James seen the article in
the newspaper? Would he decide that my being a quint
was a bigger deal than he'd thought? He might not
want to hang out with me anymore.

In the next few days I talked with him a couple of
times but he never said anything about the article. I had
to know, so finally I flat out asked him if he'd seen it.

"Sure I did," he said. "Your school picture doesn't
do you justice. You're prettier than that."

That made me feel good, but still, I had to know
his true feelings. "You don't mind . . . that people . . .
that I'm . . . ?"

"Look, Emma, all I care about is you. You haven't
changed."

"Oh," was all I could say. We went on talking, but in
a corner of my mind I was thinking this was a break-
through. To James, at least, I was simply Emma. It was
a small start, true, but still a start. I could go on from
there.

CHAPTER 18

On the second Saturday in June Gypsy and I were at drama class as usual.

Helen barged in a little late, looking a bit flustered. She stood before us, glowing, as though she had wonderful news.

"Thespians . . ." Her broad smile beamed at each of us. "They're going to be next Wednesday."

Most of us had a *huh?* look, but I noticed one or two with awe-struck expressions. No one said a word.

"The movie auditions," Helen said.

I felt a cold, hard lump in my middle. Oh, no. I could not do this. I could not set myself up for total humiliation.

Gypsy leaned forward with lips parted, eyes energy-activated. "Oh, my God," she breathed. "It's actually going to happen."

"If you're wondering how I know . . . well, I was told a couple of weeks ago that the auditions were coming up," Helen said. "I have contacts at the film office in the city from those long-ago days of acting back East.

Then this morning, just before I left, one of my friends called to say the auditions would be next Wednesday. That's good. It'll give you all time to brush up your acts, and you'll be able to audition while you're still on a high."

"Will they be here . . . the auditions?" Henry asked.

"No, they'll be held at the high school auditorium." Helen pulled some sheets of paper out of a big envelope. "There'll be others besides you trying out. Kids from the drama clubs of various schools."

"I thought it would be just us." That was Henry again. "You mean we'll, like, have to compete?"

"Competition is the name of the game in show business," Helen said to all of us. "You people might as well face that now if you want to go on with it."

Gypsy whispered to me, "The wimp probably thought he had a part nailed down. He should be so lucky."

"Today we're going to go through the monologues you've done before in class. Then I'll hand you some scripts and have you read cold. That means without any prior knowledge of what the script's about."

Someone mumbled, "That's not fair."

"That's the way it is," Helen said cheerfully. "Who wants to be first?" She looked around. No one volunteered. "Okay, I'll just call out a name." She took a seat behind us.

One by one we did our monologues. I was so nervous I was sure I'd never be able to get through Laura's speech from *The Glass Menagerie*. But somehow I did.

"Emma," Helen said when I was finished, "don't

rush the speech so much. Laura is unsure of herself. She's introverted, shy; she's never gone out among people. Show us that uncertainty when you say her lines. Pause now and then. Want to run through it again?"

Actually, I didn't. I glanced at Gypsy, who gave me a thumbs-up sign. Taking a deep breath, I paused as we'd been taught to do and tried to get inside the character. Shy, introverted Laura. Unsure of herself. I could certainly understand her feelings because I was all those things, standing up there.

"That was much, much better, wasn't it, class?" Helen said. The kids seemed to agree.

When everyone had finished, Helen walked to the front of the room. "For the most part, you actors are pretty polished," she said. "If they ask you to perform a monologue, do it the way you did just now. Only better."

"What do you mean, *if?*" Terri wanted to know.

"It's hard to say what they'll ask you to do," Helen said. "In case it's a cold reading, we're going to run through how to do that now. If the casting director lets you all stay in the room, you'll learn something just from watching the others. But try not to imitate anyone else. Bring something of your own to the reading."

She paused. "Most likely, you'll all be off in another room and be called in one by one. In that case, you'll have no idea what they're going to ask."

"It sounds really scary," Corliss said.

"It's absolutely terrifying," Helen said with her wide smile. "You'll wish you could dry up and disappear."

Amidst the groans someone shouted out, "That's show business."

"Right, Stacey. No one said it's easy. But if acting is what you want, you'll have to suffer through a lot of discouragement, terror, and rejection." Helen beamed another smile at us. "Now I'm going to call a name and hand you a side of a script. I'll tell you what character you're to read, and I'll do the other character in the scene. Each script is different because I want cold readings."

At that moment I began to have real doubts. Was being an actor so important to me that I was willing to put up with discouragement, terror, and rejection?

Corliss was first, then Henry. After each one, Helen told them what was good and bad about their performance, but she wouldn't let them do it over. "You only get one chance," she said.

Gypsy had her turn, followed by about five others, and then Helen called on me. My part was a girl arguing with her mother, and I tried to get some of my sister Alice into my voice. When I had finished, Helen said it was the best work I'd done yet. Flushed and happy, I went back to my seat, where Gypsy whispered, "You had it nailed. Good show." I felt a whole lot better about the auditions the next Wednesday. Maybe I was meant to be an actor after all.

I didn't meet James that day because Gypsy wanted me to go along on another moving job Kurt had lined up. So far this summer we hadn't spent a lot of time together.

"Is James heartbroken because you gave him the brush today?" Gypsy asked as we headed for our bikes.

"I think he'll survive," I said. "Anyway, it's not as though we *have* to meet every Saturday." I didn't mention that Drew was off with James somewhere.

"I brought along a couple of play books I checked out of the library," Gypsy said. "I thought we could read some scenes together while we're sitting around."

"Please, Gypsy. We just got out of class."

"So?"

"So why not give it a rest?"

Gypsy looked annoyed. "You don't sound very sold on breaking into the big time."

"I'd like to land a part in the movie."

"Oh, right. You want to be famous without putting out any real effort."

Now I was annoyed. We'd reached our bikes and I was tempted to tell Gypsy I'd changed my mind about going with her. I didn't, because I was afraid Gypsy would say "Fine" and go off alone, and that would be the end of our friendship. Gypsy's the kind of person who demands perfect loyalty.

We biked to the moving site and I was the one who suggested we start reading a scene.

We acted several different parts, and it was fun trying to figure out what the characters were really like.

Going home later, I wondered how Gypsy and I would feel if one of us got cast and not the other.

The thought of only one being chosen sent my mind

skittering to Natalie. There had been no further talk at home about her wedding plans. Would any of us go to the ceremony? It broke my heart to think of our family being divided. I guessed it must be doubly heart-breaking for Natalie.

That night I could bear it no longer. I went to Alice and Beth's room and then to the boys'. "We've got to meet," I told them. They all seemed to sense why.

It was close to midnight when we crept to Craig and Drew's room.

Craig had brought up a bag of pretzels and some sodas. After the *pop* sounds of cans being opened had died down, Craig looked at me. "Speak."

I took a swig of soda and wiped my mouth. "It's about Natalie," I said.

"I figured it would be."

"What are we going to do?" Beth's eyes were round, full of concern. "It's so awful about her and Dad. I thought after that phone call they'd made up, but it doesn't seem like it."

"It's awful for all of us. Even Natalie's mother," Alice said. "I mean, I imagine she wants her only daughter to have a big wedding. I'll bet she wishes she could divorce Dad all over again for the way he's acting, not letting the five of us take part."

I took a deep breath. "That's not what Dad and Natalie fought about. It was about me."

Four pairs of eyes stared at me. Then Drew said, "What do you have to do with it?"

I took another breath. "Natalie wanted me to be maid of honor."

The room was deathly silent. I could hear Craig's monster clock ticking.

"You?" Alice said. "Just you?"

I nodded and stared at the can of soda in my hand. Little drops of moisture were running down the side. "She said . . . if all five of us were involved, we'd get all the attention."

I was waiting for an explosion of anger, but there was only more silence. Then Beth said, "If that's what Natalie wants, what's wrong with it?" She looked subdued and a little sad, but not angry.

Alice echoed, "If that's what Natalie wants . . ."

I started crying. "But it's not fair to you guys. I knew it all along, but I didn't want to admit it."

"Oh, Emma, don't cry." My sisters scooted to each side of me and put their arms around me. That made me cry more.

"You've always been closer to Natalie," Alice said. "I can understand. Can't you, Beth?"

"Sure. It's okay, Emma. Really."

"You mean that's what Dad was so steamed about?" Craig asked.

"Yes." I reached up for the box of tissues on Drew's desk.

"And just because of that he went on a rampage?"

"He said . . ." I blew my nose. "He said that if we all couldn't take part, none of us could."

"That's Dad," Drew said. "You gotta love him."

"And then Natalie said she wasn't going to have her wedding turned into a circus."

"I don't get it," Craig said.

"She meant the press," Alice explained. "If we all were in the wedding part, it'd be front page news."

"Oh, get real," Craig said, kicking his foot against hers.

"Maybe not front page news," I said, "but it's possible we'd get more than our share of attention. I don't blame Natalie for not wanting to be upstaged at her own wedding."

There were grunts of agreement.

"So what are we going to do about it?" Beth asked. "We can't let Dad not go to his own daughter's big day. Poor Dad."

"Yeah, right. But . . ." We sat around, looking at each other, thinking. Then Alice sat up so suddenly her soda splashed. She grabbed some tissues from the box I was still holding and blotted it up.

"Why don't we call Natalie and tell her we really wish she'd go ahead with her plans for an all-out affair?" Alice said. "She can get her friends to be her attendants. And we'd just sort of scatter around the audience so no one would notice us." Coming from Miss Attention-Getter, that was quite a suggestion.

I felt just the slightest pang. I guess, in spite of everything, I'd held on to that mental image of me being the maid of honor.

Beth was saying, "No, let's not call. Let's write a letter. That way we can say it right and not get carried away like we might do on the phone."

We all agreed. Beth got some flowery stationery. Among us, we composed a letter that said we wanted Natalie to have a perfect wedding and how we planned to fade into the scenery. It wasn't any literary master-piece, but it sounded sincere. We all signed it.

After that, we sat around and talked. I couldn't remember the last time I'd felt this close to my siblings. If I had to be a quint, I couldn't have picked a better bunch to be . . . well, bunched with, I thought. The boys were more sensitive than I'd given them credit for. As for my sisters . . . who'd have thought they could be so unselfish?

"Guys," I said, feeling tears in my voice, "I love you." I was taking a chance, risking remarks.

Instead, silently, everyone reached out to those on either side, and we sat in a circle of love, quint style.

CHAPTER 19

On Wednesday morning I was awakened by the phone.

"Are you nervous?" Gypsy asked.

"I am now."

"Oh, did I wake you up? How could you sleep when our future is about to begin? I'm a bundle of nerves," Gypsy said. "Listen, how are you going to get to the auditorium?"

I hadn't thought about it. "Bikes?"

"Too lowbrow. So is Kurt's truck, but he offered to drive us. We could get out before anyone sees us."

"Would you pick me up at the corner?" I asked. "No one knows I'm going to audition today, except James. Now I wish I hadn't even told him."

"How come?"

"What if I don't get a part? I'll feel so stupid."

After a pause Gypsy said, "Emma, if you're serious about acting you'll need to toughen up."

Instead of replying that I might not be all that serious, I said, "I wonder if Helen will be there. I can't imagine

167

her missing it. Maybe she'll sit out in the auditorium with the director and whisper little things in his ear, like, 'That girl is loaded with talent.' "

"I wonder how many kids will be trying out," Gypsy said. "I wouldn't be surprised if more than fifty show up, when you consider the drama clubs in all the schools. Of course, not everyone will want to try out." Gypsy paused. "Although I can't imagine anyone in their right mind not jumping at the chance to be in a real movie."

"If there's fifty, we can kiss our chances good-bye," I said, and then added quickly, "I mean me, not you."

We decided that, instead of waiting, I'd ride my bike to Gypsy's right away. Then we'd have time to practice our monologues.

When I came downstairs I saw my parents had already left for work. Dad's newspaper was lying on the table. While I spooned up cereal, I turned to my favorite gossip column in the paper, written by a couple of women. Some days there was good stuff about celebrities, mostly film stars.

Today there wasn't much of interest, just an item about a judge who took bribes and another about an alderman who went on too many trips. But then—then my glance landed on a brief paragraph near the bottom. Oh, no!

Open auditions are being held today for young teens interested in appearing in Kankakee, *a movie to be shot mainly in suburban Stevensville. Today's tryouts for bit parts will be held at the Willard High School Auditorium, starting at one P.M.*

Oh, thanks a lot! Open auditions meant anyone could come and try out. So there'd probably be kids who didn't know the first thing about acting . . . who just wanted to be in a movie!

I tore out the item to show to Gypsy and left it on the table to pick up on my way out. Now I wasn't so much nervous as angry.

Helen had suggested that instead of getting dressed up we wear regular clothes. "They're looking for real kids, not phonies," she'd told us.

I decided to try to look sharp in a casual kind of way. I'd wear a trace of make-up . . . just enough to heighten my coloring.

Jeans. I'd wear jeans, the pair with tiny tucks around the waist. The top was harder to decide. I riffled through everything in my closet and then went into my sisters' room and looked through their stuff.

Alice was still snoozing, but Beth glanced up from a book she was reading in bed. "What's up?"

"I'm trying to find something outstanding but under-stated."

"Want to wear my new red?" She shifted and propped her head up with her hand.

"You wouldn't mind?"

"No, go ahead." Beth turned back to her book.

"Thanks!" I patted my sister's head and went through the bathroom into my own room. The top was really cute, with an appliquéd arrow design coming down from the yoke. It went great with the jeans. Sometimes sisters can be so sweet and unselfish!

I thought my look was just right until later on when

I saw Gypsy, and then I felt like Miss Prep School. She was wearing old jeans and an oversized T-shirt knotted at the side. With her hair piled up on top of her head and enormous dark glasses hiding her eyes she looked the way I imagined real actresses did at big-time auditions.

"Maybe we should get there a little early," I said to Gypsy. "Remember Helen said they'd probably hand out numbers as we arrive?" I leaned toward the mirror to comb my hair. "Oh, and you know what? There was an item in the paper . . ." And then I remembered I'd left it lying on the kitchen table. "It said the auditions would be open."

"Today?"

"Yes, today. So it looks like just anyone can show up and try out."

"Let's go," Gypsy said. "I don't want to be at the tag end if lots of goon girls show up. I'll get Kurt."

We had to take Raven and Sasha along on the ride because there was no one at the house to watch them. Sasha sat on Gypsy's lap and Raven on mine. We had only the cab seat of the truck and there was no way the girls could be trusted to ride in the open bed.

As he drove us over, Kurt couldn't resist making heavy-handed remarks about how we should remember him when we became rich and famous film stars. Gypsy said, "I could forget you next week if you weren't around."

"You don't mean that, kid."

"Try me." To be decent she added, "Just kidding," but a nudge in my ribs told me she wasn't. She leaned forward to look at a street sign. "You can let us out here, Kurt."

We started walking. As we rounded the corner of the last block we both gasped. Kids! They were standing in bunches all over the front lawn of the school. Other kids had draped themselves along the low wall by the sidewalk, and a big crowd waited on the steps. And more kids were arriving every minute as cars pulled up and disgorged as many as six or seven at a time.

Gypsy and I stared in horror at the mob scene and then at each other. We couldn't believe it. There had to be a couple of hundred kids milling around.

I turned to go. Gypsy grabbed my wrist.

"Listen, Emma, we've got as good a chance as anyone. Better. We're prepared. Don't pull a fade on me now."

"But . . . but . . ." I thought of the worst possible thing. "What if they let everyone sit in the audience and watch?"

"So? You'd be watching them, too."

"I'm scared, Gypsy."

"A little stage fright will give an edge to your audition." She surged forward and I followed. To the first bunch of kids she said, "You guys here for the tryouts?"

"What do you think?" A girl held up a card with *238* printed on it. "You've gotta go up by the door and get a number."

As we pushed our way through the crowd, I saw lots of kids I knew. I doubted that many, if any, had an ambition to act. They just wanted to be in a movie.

The woman passing out the numbered cards looked as though she wished this were some other day.

My number was 445. Gypsy's was 444.

"How long do you think it'll take to get to us?" Gypsy asked the woman.

She pulled her look away from the crowd. "God only knows. One or two hours." Wearily, she pushed her hair behind her ears. "They're going to take them in by twenties. You figure it out."

"Thanks for those encouraging words," Gypsy said innocently. She lowered her sunglasses to stare at some kids across the way, under a big tree. "Aren't those your sisters over there?"

I moved to get a better view. It was! "What are *they* doing here?"

"The same as everyone else. Want to amble over?"

"No." Great, just great. My own sisters competing against me.

I felt a heavy hand on my shoulder and turned. Helen!

"How's it going, girls?"

I made a face.

"We didn't expect these hordes of kids," Gypsy said. "We thought it would just be our class and the drama clubs."

"Yes," I said. "It isn't fair."

"Why not?" Helen was smiling broadly as usual.

"Because they wouldn't even have known about the auditions if it hadn't been for that item in the paper." I realized my sisters must have seen it there on the kitchen table.

"It's competition," Helen said. "That's the way it is in show business—and lots of other fields, too. You'll just have to get used to it." She looked around at the crowd. "Sometimes you don't have to be all that talented—you just have to be there." She spotted Terri and Henry. "I'll go cheer my people on. See you girls inside."

As we watched her plowing her way through the clumps of kids, Gypsy said, "It kinda makes you wonder why we bothered to learn acting, doesn't it? But maybe we'll have a special shine that'll make us stand out."

We heard a loudspeaker and then made out the words: "Quiet, please, everybody. Numbers one through twenty move over to the side door. Numbers twenty-one to forty come up and be ready."

I felt a little tremble of excitement. The auditions were beginning!

"Are you nervous?" I asked Gypsy.

"Not yet. Not until they get to the four hundreds."

Two young women came out on the steps and told us all to start lining up. One called out numbers and the other got us into order. Gypsy and I were halfway down the block.

Gypsy nudged me and nodded toward the girls in front of us. They were with a woman who must have been the mother of one of them. "Look . . . they've got composites," she whispered.

"What?" I whispered back.

"Professional photos. Eight-by-ten glossies."

I sneaked a look. Each girl was holding a page of

photos of herself . . . one close-up and others showing her in a dance outfit or gym outfit or just standing around looking spiffy.

Gypsy turned her back to them so they couldn't hear. "Blast that Helen," she whispered. "She didn't tell us to bring photos."

"I don't have any like those," I whispered back. "Do you?"

"Well, no, but any picture would help. How are the casting people going to remember us out of all these kids?"

Our line moved in spurts. We got to the front of the building and finally curved around toward the side door. When there were maybe forty or fifty kids ahead of us, one of the young women came along and checked our numbers and then handed out cards. Ours were pink and the boys' were blue.

"How awfully sweet," Gypsy said. "Just like a baby shower."

"While you're waiting, fill these out," the young woman snapped. If she was from Hollywood, she didn't look it. She had a bad complexion and an even worse attitude.

The card asked the usual stuff: name, address, phone number, age. There were spaces for a Social Security number and sizes, and then it asked if you had a dog, casual and dressy clothing, and any special abilities.

"What special abilities do we have?" Gypsy asked me.

"Catching parrots?" I suggested.

"I can't think of a thing. Oh! Acting! We can act!"

"Wouldn't it sound . . . I don't know . . . show-offy if we said that?" I asked.

"If we don't, who will?"

Gypsy wrote it down, but I didn't. I'd let them decide whether I could act or not. I started getting butterflies in my stomach.

We were now very close to the door. The butterflies were in a frenzy. "I'm so scared," I said.

"That's good. Like I said before, it'll sharpen your performance."

I tried to remember the lines of my monologue. I couldn't think of the opening. I felt panicked.

Now we were inside. When my eyes adjusted from the sunshine to the dimness in the backstage area, I could see kids ranged along the stage. I could hear someone speaking but couldn't make out the words.

"Okay," a guy standing nearby in sweats and running shoes said to us. "Four hundred forty to sixty, go out on the stage."

My legs felt boneless as I walked behind Gypsy. We stood in a row across the stage. I could see two people —a man and a woman—in the seats down below. There were others sitting farther back. Helen had to be out there somewhere. I hoped I wouldn't disgrace her.

"Give me your names and ages," the man said. "Project your voices."

We did.

"Thank you. Now as you go off, give your card and photo to Jody over there. If you don't have a photo, go over to the white sheet offstage right and be photographed. We'll call you in two or three days if you're selected."

I couldn't believe it. This was all? This was what we'd practiced for?

Gypsy and I got in the photo line. When my turn came, the guy said, "Sweetheart, could you smile a little? This isn't a public hanging."

Outside, Gypsy and I looked at each other. "Well, damn," she said. "What a lot of nothing."

"We don't have a chance," I said. "Unless they just happen to be looking for our types."

"Yeah, sure. Like we're going to stand out from all those smartasses with their composites."

Still, I had a glimmer of hope. I could get lucky. It could happen. But then, it could also happen to Alice or Beth.

We talked about it that night in their room. We all said we didn't have a chance, but I noticed that none of us talked for long on the phone. We knew it was too soon to hear from the movie people, but . . . well, you never could tell. As Alice said, "If they saw someone for certain that they wanted, they might call up right away."

We waited the next day and the day after and the day after that. The call never came. It never came for Gypsy, either.

CHAPTER 20

*M*y sisters laughed, as though the tryouts had been just a fun adventure, but I was hugely disappointed. It surprised me to realize how much I'd counted on being in this movie.

James told me that from the way I'd described them, the tryouts had been like a lottery, completely beyond my control. That was some consolation . . . until Gypsy called.

"Guess what," she said. "Dolores got chosen."

A knife twisted in my gut. "Dolores?"

"Yeah. Not surprising. She was good in class."

"Right. But how would the casting agent know that?"

"They called back about thirty kids and actually had them read some lines. Dolores wowed them, I guess."

"How do you know all this, Gypsy?" Maybe it wasn't true.

"I called Helen. She all but confessed that she's the one who got them to give Dolores the callback."

"That's not fair!" I kicked off my shoes so hard one banged against the wall. "Teachers shouldn't play favorites."

"The guys probably asked her if she knew anyone talented . . ."

"You're talented," I said, expecting Gypsy to reply, "So are you."

Instead, she went on about the breaks of show business. I didn't want to hear that stuff. I just wanted to go on about the unfairness of Helen and her precious Dolores. I wondered if the two of them could possibly be related. Well, no, probably not. But Helen should have recommended someone besides just Dolores. Me, for example.

*　*　*

We got a letter back from Natalie, addressed to all of us. She said she was touched by our offer to fade into the woodwork. It made her realize how important we were to her, she went on, and she really couldn't imagine getting married without all of us around to lend moral support. She and Noel wanted us as bridesmaids and ushers. They'd rope in a pair of friends as maid of honor and best man.

Again I felt that twinge of regret about losing out on being the maid of honor, but I knew this was the only way to go. Maybe someday I'd get to play the role at Beth's or Alice's wedding.

We showed the letter to Mom and Dad.

"Well?" Craig asked as Dad finished reading.

"If that's what everyone wants," he said, "it's fine with me. I don't like to interfere in things like this."

Even Mom rolled her eyes.

"What'll we wear?" Alice wondered. "Should we call Natalie and find out?"

"Good idea," Mom said. "The wedding's only . . . oh, give me strength . . . six weeks off!"

Natalie said she had her gown already and she wouldn't mind flying in to help us pick out dresses. "I might as well take advantage of Dad's flying privileges while I'm still his daughter," she said. And hastily added, "Unmarried daughter."

I had the impression that she also wanted to make up with him, to smooth over hurt feelings and start fresh. I'm sure Dad wanted that, too.

* * *

I couldn't decide whether to go back to drama class or not. I mean, what was the point? If people were going to be picked for parts just because they *could act* . . . I felt funny, thinking this. What had I thought up to now? That I could be an actor because I was . . . let's not be modest now, Emma . . . cute?

But then, I reasoned, what was wrong with that? I was willing to bet that lots of kids landed in sitcoms and commercials and movies, too, just because they were attractive. Even dogs—yes, the four-legged kind —could be taught to act. So go figure.

I was thinking these heady thoughts on Friday while walking into a stationery store to look for a birthday card. And who should I run smack into but Helen. She looked bright and cheery, as always.

"Emma! How nice to see you!" She positively beamed.

"Hi." There was no way I could leap around her without being downright rude.

"All set for class tomorrow? You have that side memorized?"

"I'm not sure I'm coming to class anymore." This just popped out.

"Oh?"

I looked away from Helen's big, open face. Why had I said that?

"Going on vacation?" she asked.

"No. I just . . . I've just lost interest in acting."

"That surprises me. You were coming along nicely."

She was waiting for an explanation. What could I say?

"I don't think I'm good enough," I said softly.

"Well, of course you're not. No one ever is. Even experienced actors go on learning, learning, learning." She stopped smiling. Her eyes, no longer buried in jolly creases, fixed me with a look. "Is acting important to you, Emma?"

"Well, yes, of course."

"Or are you just going along with your friend Gypsy?"

"We both want to act," I said.

"I see. Well, if you're determined, nothing, no one, will stop you. If you're really passionate, you'll make it. If not . . ." She shrugged. "There are other things in life."

I didn't know what to say, but with Helen that was never a problem.

"Personally, I'd rather live life than act it," she went

on. "There are so many mind-boggling things to do!" Her eyes started to crinkle again. "And you, Emma, how I envy you . . . just starting out and so many options!"

As I was about to say, "Like what?" Helen waved to a woman across the store. She started away, then turned to me again and said, "Come back, finish what you started. Then begin your search. You're a neat kid. I expect to be hearing from you."

As I watched her walk away, I was confused for a second. Did Helen mean I should keep in touch? No, I didn't think so. She wasn't the cozy kind. Could she mean that I was . . . that I could . . . ? A little tingle went up my back. *Helen thought I had something to offer to the world.* Me . . . Emma . . . the girl, not the quint!

* * *

That night when I talked with Gypsy I didn't mention that I'd run into Helen or that I'd been thinking of ditching class. Realistically, it would look like sour grapes if I didn't show up. Also, I was curious about Dolores. Would she suddenly have that aura they say stars possess? If so, I certainly wanted to see it.

At class on Saturday I saw that so far fame hadn't put its mark on Dolores. She appeared as colorless as always.

Helen let us talk for a while about the audition. Most of the class complained about the number of kids competing.

"I admit it was a cattle call," Helen said. "Surprised

me, too, but that's how it goes sometimes. At least you've had that experience. Now let's put all that behind us and get to work."

Something had gone out of the class for me. For the first time I found it boring. I was glad when it was over and Gypsy, Drew, James, and I could go Rollerblading.

In spite of her newness to the blades, Gypsy wheeled up and down the street without losing her balance once.

James and I were watching her and Drew when suddenly a guy got out of a car and came toward us. "You kids live here?" he asked.

I glanced around to see if by some miracle a squad car was hovering about. There was none. "C'mon, James," I said, touching his arm, and we started away.

"Hey, wait!" the guy called out. "I'm a talent scout!"

"Sure you are," James said.

Drew and Gypsy came rolling up. Safety in numbers, I thought. We let the man catch up with us.

He pulled a card from his pocket. "I'm with the *Kankakee* company," he said. "In one of the street scenes, it calls for some kids to go skateboarding through the crowd. But seeing you guys, I guess those—what do you call them?—are more current."

"Rollerblades," Gypsy said.

"Whatever. If you're interested, be ready to show up on this date." He scribbled it on the card. "But before that, call this number and say that I've talked to you. They'll give you instructions."

We watched the man leave, and then looked at one another, open-mouthed. *Be prepared,* Helen had said.

But who'd have thought skating would be the thing that started us on the road to fame? Gypsy pocketed the card and we went into a frenzy of skating. Wow! Even if all anyone saw of us in the movie was a quick shot of us dodging through the crowd, we'd still have done it!

That night at dinner when Drew and I broke the news, Alice said, "You'll just be blurs, you know. Blobs on the screen."

"Don't be so sweet," Drew said. "You'll spoil us."

"When's this going to happen?" Dad wanted to know. "Maybe I'll take the day off."

Neither Drew nor I had checked the card. I called Gypsy. "The twentieth of August," she said.

My heart turned into a giant dough ball. August twentieth was my sister's wedding day.

Gypsy kept advising me not to feel bad. "Being in a wedding is more important than being in a mob scene where they probably won't even show your face," she said.

When I called James, he loyally said that if I couldn't be there, he wouldn't be in the scene, either.

"Don't be silly," I told him. "This could be your big break."

"I'm not interested in acting," he said. "I was just going along because you wanted to do it."

"Please do it anyway," I told him, "and keep Gypsy company. Later on we'll all have something to talk about."

As the days went by, the movie seemed less and less important. I was thinking more and more about the wedding and waiting anxiously for Natalie to come as she'd promised. Finally she did.

When I saw my sister, the split-second image of me on the screen faded entirely away. The wedding was one of the biggest events in Natalie's life and it would rate star billing in mine, too.

She could stay only a couple of days, so the shopping was frantic, but satisfying. The dresses, waltz length, were pale blue, a color that looked good on all of us. We'd each wear our hair pulled back with a big bow, and we'd carry white roses.

Natalie wanted to take Mom and Dad out to dinner the last night, but Mom said no, it should just be father and daughter. It brought tears to my eyes to think of Dad, and how he was giving up his firstborn, in a way. And then I wondered if he'd feel nostalgic when the rest of us got married. He'd probably go out and celebrate for a month.

* * *

Natalie shared the bed in my room, as she often did when she came home. We lay talking in the dark for a long time. I asked her a lot of stuff about Noel and she told me everything I wanted to know.

"You two are very lucky," I said. "Your life will be so perfect."

"C'mon, Emma, no one's life is perfect," she said. "It'd be kind of boring if nothing upsetting ever happened."

I rose up on my elbow. "Mom said something like that one time."

"Well, she's right."

I flopped back down. We were quiet for a while. I supposed Natalie was thinking about the wedding, but she said, "How's the acting going? Is it still as exciting?"

"Not really. I don't feel"—I remembered Helen's word—"passionate about it."

"Oh?"

"I think it was Gypsy who made me think I was interested. And I told myself I really was. But now I don't feel that acting's all that important to me."

"Then give it up."

"You wouldn't think I was a wimpy quitter?"

"Of course not, Emma. You're just beginning. You've got to try things . . . different things . . . to see where your passions, as you put it, lie."

I sighed. "I wish I knew now. All I know is that I want to be somebody. You know what I mean? Someone who, well, maybe not stands out in the crowd, but . . ."

"Knows who she is?"

"Right. Even if . . . if nobody else knows."

"They'll know, Emma. Believe me."

"I worry about next year. High school. I'm so afraid I'll get lost."

"Lost?"

"Not physically, although probably that, too. I mean . . . all five of us will be in the same school. I may be lost in quintville."

"Only if you let yourself be."

"How can I avoid it?"

"That's up to you. Look, Emma. The folks protected you guys when you were young and tender. They didn't let you be exploited. But now you have wings. You're on your own. It's up to you where you fly."

"Yeah." I felt a little dreamy. I could see all the kids I knew—Gypsy, James, Dolores, and the rest of them, my brothers and sisters included—taking off from the same branch but flying in different directions. Where would we all go? The horizon was far and wide.

"Natalie?"

"Ummm?" Her voice was dreamy, too.

"How do you picture me, when you think of me?"

"I picture you as my darling Emma. My sister."

"But . . . can you see me as something more? I mean . . ." *Tell me, Natalie,* I thought, *what direction I should take.*

"You'll be someone," she said sleepily, with a yawn. "You already are. Just follow your instincts . . . your heart."

For a brief moment I wondered if by "Follow your heart" she meant romantically, as she had with Noel. No, I didn't think so. I think she meant I should follow wherever my passions led me. I would. I would. But there was time.

I yawned and settled down on my pillow. "Good night, Natalie," I said.

"Good night, little sister. Mmmm." She was asleep.

"Be happy," I whispered. I meant that for Natalie. But I also meant it for us . . . all us kids who were about to find our way in the world that was waiting out there.